1973

Books by GEORGE HARMON COXE

Murder with Pictures (1935)

The Barotique Mystery (1936)   *The Camera Clue* (1937)

Four Frightened Women (1939)

Murder for the Asking (1939)   *The Glass Triangle* (1939)

The Lady is Afraid (1940)   *No Time to Kill* (1941)

Mrs. Murdock Takes a Case (1941)

Silent Are the Dead (1942)   *Assignment in Guiana* (1942)

The Charred Witness (1942)

Alias the Dead (1943)   *Murder for Two* (1943)

Murder in Havana (1943)   *The Groom Lay Dead* (1944)

The Jade Venus (1945)

Woman at Bay (1945)   *Dangerous Legacy* (1946)

The Fifth Key (1947)   *Fashioned for Murder* (1947)

Venturous Lady (1948)

The Hollow Needle (1948)   *Lady Killer* (1949)

Inland Passage (1949)   *Eye Witness* (1950)

The Frightened Fiancée (1950)   *The Widow Had a Gun* (1951)

The Man Who Died Twice (1951)

Never Bet Your Life (1952)   *The Crimson Clue* (1953)

Uninvited Guest (1953)   *Focus on Murder* (1954)

Death at the Isthmus (1954)   *Top Assignment* (1955)

Suddenly a Widow (1956)   *Man on a Rope* (1956)

Murder on Their Minds (1957)

THESE ARE BORZOI BOOKS, PUBLISHED IN NEW YORK BY

ALFRED A. KNOPF

MURDER ON THEIR MINDS

*A confidential report missing, a news-photographer black-
jacked, a girl mugged, one of Boston's most Olympian fam-
ilies secretly investigated, an ex-cop killed. Which of these
things related to one another? Which were blind alleys?
Kent Murdock of the* Courier *had asked to be put full-time
on the case. Tom Brady, the murdered man, had been
a friend of his. Walt Carey, the newsman who'd been
slugged, was another. And tawny, striking Rita Alderson,
who'd asked Kent's help before it all began, wanted to be
a third.*

*The missing report was the key. Tom Brady's letter made
that clear: "No question about this being the biggest case
I ever worked on," it began. "But when I think of the trouble I'm making for a lot of people sometimes I wish I hadn't
started." The thing he hadn't known was the trouble he'd
started for himself.*

*Kent Murdock is probably mysterydom's most popular
news-photographer, and George Harmon Coxe certainly
one of our most popular mystery writers. Together they
make a combination that's hard to beat.*

GEORGE HARMON COXE

Murder on Their Minds

1 9 5 7

ALFRED · A · KNOPF   NEW YORK

L. C. CATALOG CARD NUMBER 57–5304

© GEORGE HARMON COXE, 1957

THIS IS A BORZOI BOOK
PUBLISHED BY ALFRED A. KNOPF, INC.

FIRST EDITION

MURDER ON THEIR MINDS

1

THE *Courier* Building stands at the intersection of two narrow streets, one of which has been designated as one-way while the other bounds the front of the structure and continues on to flank the loading platforms and the company parking lot beyond. Kent Murdock, the *Courier's* picture chief the past few years, was cutting across the angle of this intersection on his way to his office when he heard the "beep" of an automobile horn accompanied by a woman's voice that called his name.

Stopping with one foot on the curb, he glanced to his right, seeing the blue sedan opposite and recognizing at once the blonde that looked out at him from the lowered window on the driver's side. It was a pretty face, and young, smiling now that his attention had been secured. He grinned back, making a small salute and then, because the traffic was steady on this late-spring afternoon and the clearance meager, he crossed behind the car and came up to open the opposite door.

"Hi, Rita," he said as he slid in beside her. "Waiting for me?"

"They told me upstairs you probably wouldn't be long. They said I could wait but—"

He chuckled when she hesitated, aware that as a waiting room the studio—a term used to designate the photo-
graphic department—was both uninviting and uncomfortable. He also understood the invitation, since it was seldom
that the studio had a visitor as easy to look at as Rita
Alderson.

"Yes," he said. "I don't blame you."

"So"—she smiled again—"I thought I'd try to catch you
here."

He waited, wondering now just why she should come
at all, for though he had known her for some time the re-
lationship was tenuous and existed because of her husband, who had been a long-time friend of his before his
death in an auto crash three months earlier.

They had been driving down the South Shore after a
Saturday night party—George and Rita Alderson—with
Rita at the wheel. There had been some low-lying fog in
spots and coming into a curve the lights of an approaching
car apparently blinded her. The inquest showed that the
speed was moderate at the time the car hit the tree, but
as sometimes happens the result was difficult to understand. For while the man was killed instantly, the woman
escaped with minor abrasions and a twisted ankle. Because Murdock had thought so often about this during the
past weeks, he gave his attention to the girl, aware that
she was looking out the windshield at the car ahead, her
hands on the wheel and a certain tension in the frown that
puckered the corners of her eyes.

He did not help her and presently, still not looking at
him, she said: "I thought—"

She stopped again and whatever it was she was thinking
seemed to be giving her a hard time. She tried again.

"It's about that detective you recommended to Harriett Alderson."

"Tom Brady?"

"He's back in town."

"Oh?"

Murdock waited, still wondering about her concern. When she did not continue he corrected her. He said it was Arthur Enders, the Alderson attorney, who had actually suggested Brady.

"But you—well, you're sort of a friend of the family, and Harriett asked you about him, didn't she?"

"I told her if she wanted a really honest private detective she couldn't do better than Tom Brady."

"Yes. And I thought—what I mean is—I heard he was coming here to have you take some pictures. Maybe not pictures exactly, but to make copies of certain papers."

Murdock said it was news to him. He said he hadn't heard about it. "I haven't seen Tom in a month," he added.

"He said there were some things he wanted to put on film," she continued, "so he'd have a permanent record of them. So I thought maybe, since you're a friend of mine —you are, aren't you?"

Murdock was still confused but he was beginning to get an inkling of what might be in the back of her mind. The inference that followed bothered him. He wondered if he should try to stop her before she committed herself, but it was difficult to concentrate now because she was looking right at him and her eyes had a quality that most men found compelling.

He saw that she wore a tailored navy dress and a black cloth coat, with a matching bit of felt topping her blonde hair. Having seen her in a bathing suit he knew that her figure was exciting, the legs straight and well shaped, her slenderness amply rounded in the proper places. Her face, which was rather long, with a full mouth and noticeable cheekbones, had a certain prettiness that had always seemed somewhat ordinary to Murdock until he remembered her eyes. Dark blue and well spaced, the black lashes startling in their thickness, they had a direct and somehow ingenuous quality that made one forget everything else at the time, exerting a queer sort of fascination that was difficult to ignore and giving the impression that, at the moment, you were the only guy in the world.

Because Murdock felt the pull of her glance as she waited for him to reply, he looked away as he answered her question. He said he liked to think he was her friend.

"And if you take pictures," she said quickly, "you have to see what you're taking. I mean, you'd know what the papers—or whatever they are—say, wouldn't you?"

Murdock found his pack of cigarettes. When she refused he lit his own. Certain now of what she had in mind, he decided it was time to stop her before they both became embarrassed.

"I know he's doing some work for Harriett Alderson," he said. "I know he's been out of town and I haven't seen him since he's been back. In fact, I didn't know he was back so I don't know anything about taking any pictures for him."

He hesitated, still conscious of her gaze and feeling his way along. "But if you're right about that I have an idea the only reason he'd come to me—after all, there are plenty of commercial photographers around—is because we're old friends and he knows he can trust me."

"Naturally."

"I imagine these papers you speak of are confidential, aren't they?"

"Well—I suppose they are."

"And if Harriett Alderson is paying him she's entitled to see his reports first, isn't she? . . . So why don't you see Brady himself?"

"I'm going to—later. But I thought if I could get some idea of just what—"

She let the word trail and there was a sag in her shoulders as her hands slipped from the wheel to her lap. Once again she was staring out the windshield and when she spoke her voice was quiet and defeated.

"You're right, of course. I shouldn't have come. I guess I'm not very bright about a lot of things. I get carried away by some stupid impulse without stopping to think."

"Lots of people do."

"I guess I didn't realize that if you told me what the papers were about you'd be cheating on a friend. So can we forget it?" She sat up and pressed hard on the starter. "Can we pretend I never came?"

She turned to him before he could reply, her smile spurious but her tone once again animated.

"We're still friends, aren't we?"

"Sure."

"I'm glad." She put her hand on his knee. "I'm not likely to forget how much you helped me after the—accident. . . . Thanks, Kent," she said.

"Thanks?" he said, reaching for the door handle.

"For not letting me spoil it."

She backed up as he closed the door, cut the wheel hard. Her front bumper kissed the one ahead of her as she angled into the street, and Murdock watched her straighten out, a frown warping his bony face and his dark eyes thoughtful.

For another moment he stood there, a lean, straight-standing man in a well-cut, lightweight raincoat; for it was cool for this time of year and overhead the sky was overcast, the breeze whipping straight in from Georges Bank to carry with it the smell of rain on the way. Oblivious now of the traffic in the street, as well as the ebb and flow of overalled men from the mechanical departments who were sneaking over to the near-by tavern to take on a quick beer, he considered again the girl and her odd mission until he realized he was wasting his time. Then, grunting softly, he quickly crossed the street.

2

THE STUDIO at the *Courier*—which published morning, evening, and Sunday—consisted of a series of rooms connected by a poorly lighted corridor which led from the anteroom to the printing room and continued on to double back and give access to the four developing cubicles.

Glass-and-wood partitions had been erected in one corner of the anteroom to include one of the two windows and form a cubby which served as Murdock's office. Inside there was room for a desk with its chair, a small table at one end of the desk, a visitor's chair at the other. A tier of green metal filing cabinets was tucked in one corner, and since there was no more floor space all other equipment had to be stacked vertically: the table holding a duplicate of the two-way radio in the city room, the monitor, which indicated which of the five company radio cars was in use, balanced on top of the radio.

The anteroom had but one occupant as Murdock came

in, a photographer named Klime who was off at four and was at the moment putting on his coat. Klime, who was not adverse to picking up a little overtime when he could, wanted to know if Murdock had anything more and Murdock said he would look.

A glance at the monitor told him three cars were in use and there was nothing in the assignment book that needed immediate attention. A quick check with the city desk assured him that things were under control, so he passed the word to Klime, shucked off his coat, and squeezed into his chair. He had no more than settled himself when a movement at his elbow caught his eye and he glanced round to find Tom Brady blocking the doorway, a briefcase in his hand.

Murdock's grin was quick and genuine. "Hey," he said happily. "Come in. Sit down if you can. . . . Where've you been, stranger?"

Brady leaned his weight against the doorframe and pushed back his hat, a ruddy-faced man with a shock of gray hair. Looking shorter than he was because of his thick, powerful body and neck, he had dark eyes and thick graying brows and a gruff-voiced way of speaking that was neither loud nor unpleasant. He would be sixty-two on his next birthday and he had retired a year and a half ago from the police department after thirty-eight years of service—as a beatman, plainclothesman, and detective—to open a small one-man office as a private detective. Now, as he took his time answering Murdock, his smile was broad and he had the manner of a man who was momentarily well pleased with himself.

"Travelin', son," he said. "Travelin'. Ask me where?"

"Consider yourself asked."

"San Francisco, Los Angeles, Mexico City, Miami Beach.

I even got to stop overnight with Alice and my two grandchildren."

"For free?"

"All of it. Places I never expected to see, ever. One
month, son. A straight hundred a week and all expenses,
and I had plenty. . . . Also," he said, winking, "a fat
bonus. A real fat bonus if I turn in a complete report. And
I think I have."

He moved inside to put aside the briefcase and ease his
weight down in the chair and said: "You know when I retired I didn't have a dime except my pension and my insurance, which I didn't want to touch."

"Because you spent it all educating your daughter, and
then—"

"Never mind why. You know I didn't expect to make
much at this private-eye business. I wanted to keep busy
and maybe make a few bucks to help out the pension and
to see how it would be away from all those years of rules,
regulations, and red tape. You helped me with the license
and the bond and the office furniture."

"So what? You paid me back."

"And for once," Brady said, ignoring the interruption,
"I get the kind of a job a guy dreams of like a hood dreams
of making a big score. Why? Because of the build-up you
gave me with old lady Alderson."

Recalling Harriett Alderson, Murdock chuckled at
Brady's descriptive phrase. He said he hadn't given any
big build-up.

"All I said was that I'd known you for a long time, that
you'd been an honest cop for thirty-eight years."

"She'd never seen a private investigator before," Brady
said. "She let it be known that she did not approve of the
breed, but she had this idea stuck firmly in her mind. She

had to have help, so she hired me. I'll be giving her her report tomorrow."

He opened the briefcase, took out a manila envelope—which seemed to be the only thing in it—and closed the case.

"Cast your bread upon the waters," he said. "You give me a plug with Mrs. Alderson, I give you the chance to earn some pin money." He tapped the envelope. "I have worked long and hard to get these records. I want permanent proof of them in case something happens to them. You told me once that all newspaper photographers did outside work when they got the chance. Does that still go?"

Murdock agreed that this was true and did not add that to forbid such side-line jobs would cause a bitter revolt in the shop. For just as some reporters had small publicity accounts to augment their salaries, so did photographers. As they went about their daily tasks, they picked up assignments from small advertisers, from acquaintances who wanted a wedding, a reception, or some personal milestones preserved on film. The office rule permitted such extra-curricular activity so long as it was done on the photographer's time; the other rule, that the man use his own supplies, was seldom obeyed. Murdock usually knew when one of his men was printing pictures for some personal account; he also knew that company film, paper, and flashbulbs were being used, but so long as the privilege was not abused he tried to remain blind to the practice because there had been times in his early days on the paper that he too had needed the extra income. More recently he had limited his work to an occasional wedding that could afford his price, and an infrequent assignment from some picture magazine.

"I will need fourteen negatives," Brady was saying, "and I will pay five dollars apiece."

"Forget it," Murdock said. "You can pay for the film."

"Quiet!" said Brady in his rough-voiced way. "This is not friendship, this is business. This is expense money and the old lady can well afford it. Should she complain I will tell her that the five dollars is not just to pay for the film and your time but for your co-operation as well. I will point out that this is a confidential and important job and that you are known to be a close-mouthed lad with a forgetful memory."

He hesitated, his tone more serious. "And that part is true enough. You will have to see what you photograph but you will read no more than you have to, since it is no concern of yours. That is why I came here. Can we do it now?"

Opposite the office door were two heavy steel cabinets. One of these held supplies and each man had a key to it; the other contained cameras and lenses and special equipment as well as Murdock's personal cameras. Now, taking out the Graphic and locking the cabinet, he led the way down the corridor to the table and equipment that had been put there for copying. When he had set up the camera and adjusted the lights he began to work.

From that point on it was impossible, as Brady had said, not to see what he was doing. The documents he photographed were assorted in size and character. Some were negative photostats with blackish background and the contents in white, some were copies of records, some were affidavits, two were letters.

Because the actual work was practically automatic and presented no problem, most of his mind was free to speculate and it was difficult not to. He remembered the things that Rita Alderson had said and wondered why she had been so concerned. He listened to Brady give a sketchy account of his travels, and because silence was embarrassing under the circumstances he asked who had been handling Brady's accounts while he had been away.

"Frank Kirby," Brady said. "Not that there was so much to handle."

And as he enumerated these accounts, Murdock considered Frank Kirby, who shared an office with Brady and had once been a police officer. Other than that the two men had little in common, for Kirby was closer to Murdock's age, with a record in the department that included a citation for shooting it out, while off duty, with three thugs who were holding up a delicatessen. That he had resigned later on was due to a reprimand and a transfer that he felt was unwarranted.

"He could have been a good cop," Brady said.

"What?"

"Kirby," Brady said. "If he hadn't been such a hothead he could have made sergeant."

"How's he doing on his own?"

Brady shrugged. "He makes a living and he likes being his own boss. Now and then we work on a thing together."

Murdock set up his last affidavit, and though he had tried not to keep track of his exposures or make an effort to evaluate the information he had seen, he knew what he had photographed. He did not know what the affidavits and the letters said but certain forms were in a sense self-explanatory because of their printed headings. Deliberately refusing to attach any significance to what he had done, he nevertheless knew that he had photographed two birth certificates, two marriage applications and one divorce, one affidavit from a minister and one from a justice

of the peace; there were two letters, copies of two hotel
signature cards, a police record, two job applications.

As he slipped out the film holder and turned off the lights
he saw Brady stuff the originals back in the manila envelope and now, as he turned into the corridor leading to
the printing rooms, the detective followed to wait in the
doorway.

Turning off the safelight, Murdock put the films in the
developer and set the timer. When he had put the cover
on the tank he turned the safelight back on and waited,
his mind busy in spite of himself and revolving not only
about Rita Alderson but about three other names he had
recognized, all belonging to, or associated with, the Alderson family. One was on a San Francisco marriage application; the other two were on the signature cards of a Miami
Beach hotel, though this in itself was not significant since
he had not noticed the dates or length of stay. What he
still did not understand was Rita Alderson's nervous concern or the impulse—stupid or not—that had brought her
to see him. For, to the best of his knowledge, there had
been no mention of her name nor of her maiden name—
Rita Carr.

"How much did you see?" Brady asked suddenly. "How
much do you remember?"

"Not much," Murdock said. "As a witness I could only
testify that I photographed fourteen items for a retired cop
named Thomas Brady."

Brady chuckled, still trailing as Murdock took the drip-
ping films back to the printing room and dumped them
into the big fixing tank. As he did so the telephone rang
and when he answered it a man's voice asked if Brady was
there.

"For you, Tom," he said, and then listened to a one-sided conversation that was almost entirely monosyllabic.

"Yeah. . . . What? . . . Sure. . . . Okay, right away." Brady hung up, stuffed the envelope in his coat pocket, and straightened his hat. "I gotta go," he said. "How long do you think for the films?"

"You want them dry, don't you?"

"Sure."

"Well, maybe a half hour."

"I'll tell you what you do," he said as he went back to Murdock's office to pick up his briefcase. "I'll pick 'em up later, or send for 'em. Put 'em in an envelope and write my name on it. If you have to go out, leave it here on the desk. . . . Or maybe you'd better put it in the middle drawer. I'll write a check for your services when I get back to the office and I'll have no argument from you."

And with that declaration he hooked a powerful fist that grazed Murdock's jaw playfully, winked, and was gone, nearly knocking over Walt Carey, who at that moment trudged in through the doorway, equipment case slung over one shoulder, his camera in hand.

Carey was twenty years older than Murdock and probably the best-known photographer in town. He had never done anything else nor worked for any other paper but the *Courier*. He had piled up too much severance pay for anyone to consider firing him, so he went his own unpredictable way, seldom missing an assignment and accompanied always by a breath that carried the aromatic odor of whisky. The younger men on the staff considered him a character, and in a way he was, a stocky, paunching man who wore a cap and baggy clothes, the jackets of which seemed too small and never matched the trousers. Now, with no more than a grunt as his greeting, he unshouldered his case, put the camera with it, and shuffled on into the darkroom corridor. He was still there five minutes later when the telephone rang and changed Murdock's plans.

For the message from Matt Dennis, the day city editor, informed him that a DC-3 with a wheel stuck was at present circling the airport and would probably be landing in another twenty or twenty-five minutes.

"Who've you got?" the editor demanded. "Keith Howard," he added, mentioning one of the newer reporters, "is out there now but no camera."

"Me and Carey," Murdock said. "Hold on while I check with him." He flipped an inter-com switch connecting with the developing room and asked Carey what he had.

"A couple of 'B.O. musts'," Carey said.

Murdock checked the assignment book and the monitor and then said: "Carey's working on some business office stuff, Matt. Unless you've got somebody closer I'd better duck out there myself. I'll take a radio car and keep in touch."

He reconsidered his decision as he hung up, but when he had ticked off the available photographers who were working that shift he saw that he was still the logical choice. But he remembered Brady's negatives too, and realized that there had only been time for him to clip half of them to the wires which were strung up to the left of the fixing tank where they could dry in the warm-air fan. As he hesitated, Carey came in with two films in metal clips.

"Do something for me, Walt," Murdock said. "See these seven negatives? String them up right next to these others for me, will you? And when they dry, put them in an envelope, write Tom Brady's name on it, and stick it in the middle drawer of my desk."

"Sure," Carey said. "Sure. . . . What's with you? Going to work for a change?"

Murdock told Carey about the crippled plane and Carey cursed softly. "B.O. musts," he said resentfully. "You know what I think the business office should do with them, don't you?"

"I know, Walt," Murdock said, chuckling.

"If they have to have so many pictures let them hire their own cameras."

"Sure, Walt," Murdock said, still chuckling. "Sure. Just don't forget what I told you."

3

THE AIRPORT assignment turned out happily for all concerned, but particularly for fourteen passengers and a crew of three. For nearly an hour, while the suspense built and preparations were made on the ground to take care of the casualties, the crippled DC-3 circled low over the field. When, finally, the landing could no longer be postponed, the pilot's skill, and a stroke of great good fortune that snapped the half-lowered landing wheel into its proper position the instant it took the weight of the plane, enabled all aboard to walk into the terminal unscratched.

To Murdock it seemed that he had seen a minor miracle enacted, but picture-wise the best he could do was get two shots of the crew while Keith Howard picked up a few usable quotes from some of the passengers. Howard, a collegiate-looking youth with a crew cut and an air of subdued excitement that he had been able to maintain ever since he had come to work as an office boy, was still talking about the experience as the company car rolled downtown at twenty minutes after six.

The police radio was on, and because of long practice Murdock was able to listen to the dispatcher's orders with one ear while the other was tuned in on Howard. That was how he happened to pick out a salient address, orient it instantly with his own position, and decide to follow it up while Howard was still talking.

He was only vaguely aware that the dispatcher was calling a certain division car, but he knew the address was practically around the corner and when he heard the words: "Investigate disturbance," he said: "Let's have a look," and pulled into the right-hand traffic lane as he came to the light.

"What?" said Howard.

"I think that address is Kelleher's."

"The steak house?"

"Probably only a drunk," Murdock said. "But it's sort of early for that, so let's take a quick look."

He made the turn and saw Kelleher's sign in the middle of the block. There was no indication of a disturbance as he pulled slowly past the entrance, but he double-parked and reached for his camera. As he stepped to the pavement he saw the police car make the turn behind him, so he hurried through the doorway, Howard at his heels.

Kelleher's had long been established as a good place to get steaks and chops and lobsters for anyone who was not interested in chrome, red leather, and an acre of mirrors. It had a sort of paneled, Old English atmosphere, the lighting subdued and the furniture heavy. There was no music at dinner but a trio came on around ten for those who wanted something to listen to after the theater.

The coatroom was on the left of the foyer as you entered, the restrooms opposite, but now, as Murdock went in, the coatroom was unattended and the hatcheck girl was peering through the doorway to the main room. At this hour the place was not crowded except for one spot in the middle of the room and as Murdock pushed through the fringe of onlookers he came upon the center of attraction —three men and a woman, not counting the two waiters who were holding one man, all talking at once.

Murdock did not know what it was all about yet but he did not hesitate. His camera had been automatically set at twelve feet, there was a bulb in the flash gun; the aperture was right, so all he had to do was trip the shutter. In the resulting light he noticed that Kelleher was on the left, looking down at a gun he held in his hand as though he had never seen it before. The man in the center and held by the two waiters was red faced and voluble as he shouted at the older, balding man who stood close to a buxom and painted blonde of thirty or so. Until she saw the flash she had been giving her arguments to the captive man, but Murdock changed all that.

Kelleher turned first, openmouthed but silent. The two waiters held on hard to their captive as he tried to lunge toward Murdock. The blonde also started forward as Murdock retreated. Her balding companion tried to restrain her but she shook him off, then stopped short as two uniformed policemen broke into the arena.

"Come on," they said. "Break it up. What's the trouble, Mr. Kelleher?"

Murdock had already twisted a fresh flashbulb into its socket and now, changing the focus, he stood on a chair and took his second picture. After that he retreated discreetly to the bar, which was now deserted except for a lone customer who sat unperturbed at the far end nursing a beer. Murdock glanced at him, looked again, and then walked over and took the stool next to Tom Brady.

"What're you doing here?" he said. "What's the hassle about?"

"Which question will I answer first?"

"Either."

"The blonde and her friend," said Brady in his detached way, "are having a drink at that far table by the wall when this lad comes in and walks over to them. There is some argument which I do not hear and then this newcomer takes the blonde's arm as if he's going to make her leave. She shouts at him and gives him a tussle and the one who is paying for her drink stands up and swings at him. Whereupon he yanks out the gun. The blonde hits his arm as he fires—I guess the slug went into the ceiling, luckily—and by that time the two waiters have grabbed him."

"Do you know them?"

"Never seen them before but the situation is familiar. When someone takes someone else's girl there is likely to be trouble, though generally not with a gun."

Murdock watched two more policemen enter and confer with their associates and Kelleher. Presently the three combatants were escorted from the room, trailed by Keith Howard, so Murdock slipped off the stool and started to follow. He got as far as the doorway when he felt the tap on his shoulder.

"Hey, Mac!"

The hand which had been transferred to his arm belonged to a man named Al Parenti, a gambler and promoter of sorts who had a record of arrests for assault of various degrees, but no convictions, a blue-jowled man with black brows and thinning black hair.

"Those pictures could make trouble for a friend of mine," Parenti said. "I wouldn't want them to get in the paper."

Murdock shook his arm loose, resenting the approach and Parenti's manner.

"I didn't take a picture of you."

"I'll be in it just the same. Also a lady friend of mine," Parenti said. "She's not supposed to be here, you know what I mean? It could make trouble for her and I wouldn't want that to happen. Forget you took 'em and I'll make it worth your while."

Murdock looked at him, dark eyes morose and un-friendly. It would, he knew, be a simple matter to explain that there was very little chance that either of the pictures would be printed unless one of the principals was impor-tant for some other reason. That he made no such expla-nation was due partly to Parenti's assumption that the picture could be bought at any price.

"I just take pictures, Parenti," he said. "I have nothing to say about whether they'll get printed or not."

"I wouldn't want that to happen."

"Then go talk to the city editor. He's a reasonable man. Make your pitch to him. But if I were you I wouldn't offer him money; he might have you thrown out."

He turned away before the other could reply, still smol-dering inside as he stepped out on the sidewalk. He saw then that the trio had been placed in the back seat of one of the police cars, and now Keith Howard came up and said he was going to grab a cab and follow on over to the precinct house.

"Just to see what happens," he said.

As he turned away Murdock saw the car across the

street and the familiar face of Walt Carey hanging out the window. He went over and asked how Carey happened to be there.

"I was out on a hold-up in Cambridge," Carey said. "On the way back I heard the call on the police radio and figured it was Kelleher's, so I thought I'd have a look. Was it anything?"

Murdock told him and then, remembering Tom Brady, decided he might as well eat dinner here as anywhere else. A glance at his watch told him it was twenty minutes of seven and he knew Carey did not go off duty until eight, so he handed over the two exposed film holders and asked Carey to take them into the studio and develop them.

"I'll be back before you leave," he said. "Just put the prints on my desk—two from the airport and two from here—and I'll caption them when I get there. Okay?"

His own car was still double parked so he drove it diagonally across the street to a parking lot and then called the city desk on the company radio to say where he was and what he was going to do. When he had switched off both radios, he locked the car and went back to Kelleher's.

The place was quiet now, with no sign that there had been any disturbance, and the room was beginning to fill up. Seven or eight of the bar stools were occupied but there was still an empty one at the end next to Brady and Murdock took it.

"Are you working?" he asked. "Or just drinking?"

"It's a little thing that came in this afternoon," Brady said. "Kelleher's been thinking that somebody's been chiseling or stealing his liquor. Neither Kirby nor myself are known here—the prices are a bit steep for my pocketbook—and we figured if there is any monkey business it might be better done during the rush hours. I will drink some beer and keep my eyes open until eight o'clock or so and Kirby will come and do the same around eleven, not that we expect to prove much."

"Can I buy you a drink?"

Brady spoke softly, his glance oblique as it ranged the length of the bar.

"It would be better not to," he said. "They know now you are a newspaper man and I'm thinking that if we appear too friendly our light-fingered friend may become temporarily honest."

Murdock nudged Brady to show he understood and slipped off the stool. As he looked about for a small table he noticed that Al Parenti and the lady friend he was so concerned about were no longer in the room.

It was a quarter of eight when Murdock parked the company car and walked back past the loading platforms to the entrance leading to the elevators. Here he met a youth named Jim Hughes, who was currently an office boy but had been promised the next opening on the staff. Hughes said that Carey had sent him out to get his supper and now, coming into the studio anteroom, Murdock yelled for Carey.

When there was no reply he stepped into his office, turned on the light, and leaned over the inter-com.

"Walt."

No reply.

"Hey, Carey."

Still no answer and now, wondering about the film holders he had given Carey, he realized that no prints had been left on his desk.

"Jim," he said as he stepped back into the anteroom. "When did Walt tell you to go out?"

"At seven. He said to be back at a quarter of eight because he was off at eight."

Puzzled, a frown warping his lean, dark face, Murdock turned and headed for the corridor. The printing room seemed empty at first glance but he stepped inside and then he stopped short, his breath caught and nerves contracting as he saw the crumpled figure on the floor.

Even in the gloomy half-light of the room he knew this was Carey—the cap which lay near by told him this much —and as he leaped forward he saw the metallic gleam of the small clips that were used to hold the cut film scattered on the floor.

"Walt!" he said, his voice harsh. "*Walt!*"

Then he was on his knees, a horrible emptiness growing in him, shaking a shoulder, then turning the limp form gently and reaching for a wrist. Only then did he realize that Carey was breathing, the sound of it regular but labored and wonderful to hear. He let his own breath out and swallowed the tightness from his throat. As he let go of the wrist Hughes's voice sounded behind him.

"Is that Walt? What happened?"

"How the hell do I know," Murdock said, his tone rough with reaction. "Get on the phone! Get a doctor!"

"W—what doctor?"

"Any doctor, damn it. Tell the operator; she'll know. Tell her to hurry it."

For a little while then Murdock was not sure what he should do. Anger had not yet begun to assert itself and the emotional impact remained an odd mixture of shock and gratitude as he slipped off his coat and folded it to make a pillow.

Carey lay partly on his side, one hand outstretched. Still not knowing how badly he was hurt and seeing no blood,

Murdock turned the body gently. When his fingers touched the swelling on the back of Carey's head, he pulled them back and adjusted his makeshift pillow. Straightening now and seeing again the metal clips, he began to pick them up.

Hughes was back in the doorway now, wide eyed and silent, and Murdock pushed past him and went to his office, some impulse making him open the center drawer.

When he saw no envelope here with Tom Brady's name on it he knew that it was not for this that Carey had been struck down. No one but Brady, Carey, and himself knew that there would be such an envelope there. That left Al Parenti, and now, as his thoughts focused, the anger came.

*

4

THEY STOOD silent as the two ambulance attendants lifted the still unconscious man onto the narrow stretcher and covered the form with a blanket—Murdock, Hughes, the doctor, and T. A. Wyman, who was the managing editor of the *Courier*. They waited until the stretcher was gone and then Wyman turned again to the doctor, a note of exasperation in his voice.

"You think he might have been hit with a blackjack, but you still can't say how bad he's hurt, is that it?"

The doctor put on his coat and hat. "He's got a lump on the back of his head but the scalp shows no laceration; that's why I suggested the blackjack. It's lucky he took it on the back of the head because the skull is thicker there, but it'll take X rays to tell us if there's been a fracture."

"When'll you know?" Wyman said. "Will you go along and see to it?"

The doctor nodded. He said they should know about the fracture in an hour or so.

"Suppose there's no fracture," Wyman persisted. "You still can't say when he'll recover consciousness."

"No. He's got a concussion, possibly a severe one, but there's no way of telling now whether there's been a brain injury. He might come to in the ambulance, in an hour, a day or—" He shrugged faintly and let the implication dangle. "I'd better get along."

Murdock cleared his throat. "I think I'll go too."

"If you like," the doctor said, "but there's no hurry; I doubt if you'll be able to talk to him tonight."

He went away and Wyman turned to Murdock, a chunky, broad-faced man with thick brows and a blunt, efficient manner. A cigar seemed to be an integral part of his features and his teeth were clamped on one now, half smoked and no longer alight.

"You figure the guy took all six negatives?" he asked.

"If he was an amateur he'd have to," Murdock said. "He probably wanted the two shots I'd taken at Kelleher's, but Carey also had the two I'd taken at the airport and apparently two he got in Cambridge. To be sure he got the right negatives he took them all."

Wyman removed his cigar, considered it glumly. One end had been chewed flat and after a moment he threw it into the wastebasket. "Tell me again about Al Parenti," he said, and when he had listened to Murdock repeat his story, he said: "Who do you know at the precinct house?"

"I know the lieutenant in charge of detectives."

"Call him," Wyman said. "Fill him in and let him get started on this. . . . Keep me posted," he said as he turned toward the door. "I'll be around for a couple of hours anyway."

Murdock sat down behind his desk and told the operator what he wanted. When he had his connection he asked for Lieutenant Walsh, identified himself, and told what had happened.

"Okay," Walsh said. "Can you narrow down the time?"

"It has to be between seven and eight fifteen."

"We'll see what Parenti was doing but I wouldn't count on it too much. I know the guy. If he wanted to put the slug on someone he'd probably hire it done. Until we can get some identification from Carey—how is he, anyway? He's going to be all right, isn't he?"

Murdock started to say yes; he wanted to say: "He has to be all right." But the way he felt he was afraid to speak the words aloud. He said he did not know. "The doc won't even guess when Walt will come around," he said.

"Well, we'll get on it," Walsh said. "I'll have Parenti checked and I'll send someone over to see your elevator man. There's a chance he might remember something that'll help."

Murdock put the telephone aside and slumped back in his chair, chin on chest and his dark gaze sightless and brooding. In the mirror of his mind he could still see the crumpled figure on the printing room floor and for the moment there seemed to be no help for his seemingly incurable depression. Only his smoldering anger kept his mind working and this was directed not only at Al Parenti but at his own helplessness.

He was not sure how long he sat there unmoving and inert, but the impulse to do something finally came and he reached for the telephone and spoke to the city desk. He said he was going to the hospital and that he'd take a company car. . . :

They couldn't tell him anything at the hospital when he first arrived, so he sat in the waiting room, chain smoking for half an hour until a young doctor approached on rubber-soled shoes and asked if he was Mr. Murdock.

"The brain X rays on Mr. Carey are negative," he said. "They're making the spinal tests now."

Murdock said: "Ahh—" and some obscure band inside him let go and he took a long, satisfied breath. "Is he conscious?"

"Not yet."

"Do you have an idea—"

"None at the moment, except that he's reacting well. As a guess I'd say he should come around all right. You can check with us in the morning. Until then there's not much we can do except wait and see."

Murdock felt a lot better when he got back into the car and started back toward the office. As a matter of habit he snapped on the police radio and presently there came the first of a series of instructions from the dispatcher at police headquarters.

The pattern was much the same. First the division number and a letter to designate the proper car—A-car, L-car, O-car—followed by an address and the instructions. To complete every second or third call the time of day was added, since all of this was tape recorded for possible future reference.

The rain that had been threatening all during the day finally broke with a windy violence just after Murdock left the hospital. He turned on the wipers and slowed down slightly, still listening as the dispatcher called an L-car.

"Cable and Company," he said and gave the address. "See the night watchman. . . . Nine-o-one."

The next message had to do with a citizen alarm at one of the city's police alarm boxes. The following one came from a radio car saying that a certain investigation had been completed. Then at 9:07 the call came that made Murdock sit up and pay attention.

It was the address that tipped him off but he had some luck too. He was on Columbus Avenue at the time, peering through the arc of his windshield, when the dispatcher gave a division number and said:

"A-car. Come in."

The answer came immediately and the dispatcher mentioned the address and added: "Second floor. . . . Rear. . . . Investigate. . . . Signal Y."

Murdock was not sure what signal "Y" meant but he knew that for some time the police, aware that the press often beat them to the scene of a crime, had been using a changing set of letters at the end of a message to indicate a crime of more than usual significance. Sometimes these letters were decoys, more often they had a meaning. Now, the letter "Y," added to the familiar address, brought Murdock to attention, and at almost the same moment he saw an on-coming car make a quick U turn. When his lights picked it up broadside, he knew it was a police sedan.

Murdock had to step on the throttle to keep up with the sedan, and now he steered with one hand while he reached for the company microphone to call the city desk and say where he was going.

"We got that one," the city editor said. "Do you know what signal 'Y' means?"

"No."

"You think it's hot?"

"I don't know," Murdock said. "I'll call you back."

Then he was making the left turn behind the police car, up over the railroad tracks now and seeing the black sedan wheel round the corner. When he followed, the car was already at the curb, and as he slowed down two officers ran across the sidewalk and vanished into a doorway set between an office-supply concern and an appliance store which occupied the ground floor of the three-story building.

Murdock knew there was a stairway beyond the doorway. He had been up it often. He had never climbed as high as the third floor, but he knew that on the second floor, rear, the office of Tom Brady stood on the left-hand side.

He could feel the rain pelting on his bare head as he pulled camera and equipment case from the car, and then he was in the dimly lighted entryway and taking the metal-banded stairs two at a time, trying to think what might have happened to Brady and then trying not to.

"It doesn't have to be Tom," he said to himself, and the answer to that was: "No."

Until he reached the second-floor landing and saw the line of office doors stretching in front of him. Most of these had upper panels of frosted glass and in only one of them did light shine through: the one on the left, rear.

The picture that came to Murdock as he opened the door remained with him for a long time to come. It took him a moment to realize fully what must have happened and the shock stayed with him for several minutes so that what he saw did not completely register, and what he did was automatic.

The office itself was familiar, the big room with two flat-topped desks placed back to back, the tiny conference room partitioned in one corner. In addition to the desk chairs, there were two other straight-backed chairs, a wooden settee, and a table on which two green metal filing cabinets stood side by side, and even in that first awful moment of incredulity Murdock noticed that one drawer was open and empty.

A felt hat that had rolled to one side with the sweatband visible lay on the floor some distance from a raincoat that looked as if it had been dropped there. Beyond, partly hidden by the second desk, a man lay on his back. One of the officers was kneeling beside him while the other bent over the telephone. On the settee, elbows on knees and head down, sat Frank Kirby.

For that first instant when Murdock stopped inside the door there was no sound. All three men looked at him, the two officers instantly, Frank Kirby more slowly and, it seemed, without recognition. Then, ignoring him for the moment, the kneeling officer glanced at his companion and shook his head.

"The guy is dead," he said.

"You know who he is?" the other said.

"Tom Brady. He was at Station 16 for years before he went to Headquarters. You'd better call in." He straightened and dusted his knee. He cocked his head as he looked at Murdock and his tone was grim and arbitrary. "You're Murdock, aren't you? With the *Courier*? How the hell did you get here so quick?"

"Heard the radio call," Murdock said. "Saw your car and followed you."

What he did then would have been difficult to explain, even to himself. To understand any part of the next couple of minutes he had to accept the fact that his reactions took place in a state of shock. He seemed to know that what the policeman said was true and yet some part of his mind simply rejected the thought that Tom Brady was dead. He could not yet believe this and in the emotional struggle that followed some small, superficial part of his mind went through a routine that had been developed by long years of experience.

He could see the two officers studying him with narrowed eyes. He could practically see them thinking and he knew the subject matter: should they throw him out or not? And in that moment when the decision seemed to hang by a thread he drew from his experience the one approach that seldom failed because it was based on vanity and the almost universal desire for a cop to want his picture in the paper.

The camera was already at his shoulder and now he said: "You with the telephone, move over a step, will you? . . . That's it. Okay."

The flashbulb exploded as the man obeyed and a second later Murdock was juggling the hot bulb he had ejected, rolling it on the desk and twisting a fresh bulb in place. Still moving he said: "One more," and took the second picture from a different angle.

"What are your names?" he said, taking command of the situation.

"Handy. . . . Goldman," they replied.

Then, before anything more could be said, he had backed away, slipping out the film holder and putting the camera on the settee beside Frank Kirby. He was at the door before one of the policemen yelled at him.

"Hey! Where you going?"

"I have to cut the motor on my car," he said. "I have to call the office. I'll be back in two minutes."

He was gone then, the half-hearted protest that followed

him unheeded. To stop him now someone would have to chase him and no one did. He went alone along the hall and it was here that the full emotional impact of what he had just seen caught up with him.

With his thoughts choked off, without knowing how or why Brady had been killed, his steps began to drag. "No," he said, as though the protest could make it true. "No." And though he spoke the word savagely, the sickness came.

His face was suddenly hot and damp. There was a curious weakness along his spine and his sight was blurred. Saliva welled in his mouth and he swallowed and swallowed again. He went down the stairs like a man with an insupportable burden on his back; still protesting, but silently now as he came out on the sidewalk and felt the welcome coolness of the steady rain on his face and head.

In the car he picked up the microphone of the company radio and pressed the switch. "Car 93 calling *Courier* desk. . . . Car 93 calling *Courier* desk."

There was a scratching sound and then: "Come in, car 93."

Murdock cleared his throat and spoke his piece.

"Wait a minute," the desk said. "I'll give you rewrite."

"I've got nothing to give him yet," Murdock said bitterly. "Just the name and address. It has to be murder but I don't know how. Send over for a film holder I'll leave on the front seat of the car. I'll leave the keys in it so whoever comes over can have it if he wants it. I'll keep the camera."

"Okay. You're going to stay with it?"

"As long as I can. I'll call you back."

He switched off both radios and put the film holder beside him. For another second or two he sat there, too beaten and depressed to move until he realized that very shortly

there would be other cars and other reporters crowding
about. . . .

The officer who had been on the telephone was talking
to Kirby when Murdock re-entered the office. The second
man had hunkered down beside a short-barreled revolver
which lay a foot or two from Brady's hand.

"Shot?" Murdock said.

"Once."

Murdock stopped at the edge of the desk. Because of the
angle he could not see Brady's face. He did not want to
see Brady's face. He wanted to remember it another way,
and so his glance moved on to notice physical details.

He saw the open jacket, the dark wet stain on the shirt.
The chair behind the desk had been overturned and the
second drawer on the right side, the one nearest the wall,
had been yanked out and lay upside down, its contents
scattered. Beyond, a metal wastebasket had been upset,
its original elliptical shape bent now. Spilling from it were
some torn papers and a tangled wad of narrow ribbon that
might have come from a typewriter.

For another moment Murdock stood there, his face
white around the mouth from the pressure of his jaws, his
eyes still sick. The straight dark hair that was incipiently
graying above the ears was wet and shiny now and there
were rain spots on his cheeks. It was then that the rage
began to kindle deep inside him, overriding his grief to
become a new and dominant focal point. For though he
had seen and photographed death in many forms it had
never before seemed quite so personal or outrageous, and
he seemed to know that whatever he might do now, whatever little help he might give, would be for Brady rather
than for the *Courier*.

He backed up to glance at Frank Kirby, hearing the

monotone of his voice as he answered the officer's questions.

"He was there when I came in," he said. "I didn't see the gun at first; I didn't know what had happened. I thought maybe it was his heart—until I saw the blood."

He said other things, but Murdock no longer heard him as he picked up his camera and went over to place it with his equipment case in the corner behind the door. There was a chair here with Kirby's raincoat slung over the back, a lightweight showerproof almost identical with his own. Kirby's new-looking and spotless light-gray hat had been tossed on top of it and Murdock had time to realize that both were in character, since Kirby was a dressy man who liked to buy the latest in fashions for men.

Now Murdock slipped out of his own coat, folded it, and because it was wet, put it on the floor next to his camera. He did the same with Kirby's coat, putting it on top of his and adding the hat. Then as the quick rap of approaching footsteps sounded in the hall, he sat down in the chair, folded his arms, and prepared himself for the business to follow.

5

A PRECINCT lieutenant and two detectives were the first to arrive, but before they had time to do more than glance about, Lieutenant Bacon, of Homicide, came in with his alter ego, a blocky, blunt-jawed man named Sergeant Keogh. The medical examiner was next, and as he began the routine of his examination the police photographer and fingerprint man came in to round out the official forces.

Seated as he was in the far corner behind the door, Murdock was not immediately noticed and it was Bacon who spotted him first while the precinct lieutenant was getting the story from the two uniformed men. This did not take long and he sent them on their way, telling one of them to stay at the main-floor entrance until relieved.

"To keep out the press," he said.

By that time Bacon had fixed his gray gaze on Murdock, not advancing, just standing there, a stiff-backed, beanpole of a man in a raincoat and a rain-spotted hat set squarely on his head. At the first glance he opened his mouth and annoyance brightened his eyes. Then they narrowed and his mouth closed and he was momentarily still; for he had known Murdock a long time and this was not the first occasion when he had found the photographer at the scene of a murder.

Murdock stared back at him, silent and unmoving, and now, Bacon, his expression like that of a disapproving teacher who would take care of an errant pupil at the proper time, walked over to the doctor and stood looking down while the examination continued. It did not take long. The doctor stood up and tipped one hand.

"That's all I can do here, Lieutenant," he said, and reached for his coat. "One shot. Reasonably close, I'd say. I think you'll find some powder tattooing on the shirt. At least that's what it looks like now."

"Quick?" Bacon asked.

"I'd say so."

"How long ago?"

"Not long. As a guess, less than a half hour."

Bacon watched the fingerprint man slip a pencil through

the trigger guard of the revolver and lift it to the desk.
While the lights were being set up for the photographer
he turned to Frank Kirby.

"You found him, Frank? Tell us about it. How did you
happen to come by?"

Frank Kirby was in his middle thirties, a lean, compe-
tent-looking man with gray-green eyes that were bold,
busy, and coldly observant. His hair was medium brown
and wiry, the angular, hard-jawed conformation of his face
giving him somehow a terrier's look. By nature he was both
cocky and aggressive, and if he was at times a little rough
it was the result of twelve years on the police force, most
of it spent collaring lawbreakers and delinquents less tough
than himself. Now, as he looked up at Bacon, his voice
was clipped and bitter.

"We were working on a little thing that came up this
afternoon. For Kelleher's steak house," he said, and related the story that Murdock had already heard from Tom
Brady. "I knew Tom would be finished with his trick," he
said, "so I stopped by to see if he could fill me in with
anything before I went down there at eleven."

"What time did you get here?"

"Nine or a little after. I don't know exactly."

"You must have wasted a little time," Bacon said. "We
got your call at 9:07."

"Yeah," Kirby said. "I guess you could call it wasted."
He hesitated, his face pale and shiny in the reflected glare
of the photographer's lights. "When I saw the gun and finally realized what had happened I guess I was too mad
to think straight.

"We weren't partners," he said. "We just shared the office and expenses. We weren't even very close. But you
couldn't sit across from Brady day after day and know the

kind of a guy he was and the kind of cop he used to be
without liking him. Then you walk in on a thing like this
and you don't believe it and then all you want to do is
get your hands on the guy that did it."

"Yeah," Bacon said. "A lot of us feel that way. So you
walked in. Then what?"

"I think I spotted that open file before I saw him," Kirby
said and nodded toward the table. "I knew he kept it
locked but it was open and empty—or it looked that way
from where I stood. I didn't see the gun at first. I wasn't
even thinking like that. He was on the floor. So was his hat
and coat. I thought maybe it was his heart."

"Was his coat open like that?"

"Yes. I saw the bloodstain when I bent over him but it
wasn't very big then. I yelled at him and shook him, not
knowing he was dead, and then I saw the gun."

"When did you decide he was dead?"

Kirby blinked, as though the thought had not occurred
to him. He said he didn't know.

"I couldn't find any pulse but his skin was as warm as
mine and I could see the bloodstain getting bigger. I knew
it must have just happened and I guess I got the wild idea
that maybe I could nail the guy that did it. I looked in
the conference room and then ran into the hall. It doesn't
make much sense now but—"

"That's okay," Bacon said when Kirby hesitated. "What
did you do?"

"There's only one way out of this floor and that's the
front stairs. Suppose my coming up had trapped the guy?
Maybe he was still around? That's how it hit me then so
I ran along the hall trying doors, hoping he'd ducked into
some office. But they were all locked and so I ran up to
the third floor but all the rooms were dark. Then I knew

I'd only been kidding myself. If I *had* trapped the guy he would have had time to duck out the front way while I was with Brady. I came back and called in and took off my hat and coat and sat down to wait."

Bacon nodded and flexed his lips. "Have you got a gun, Frank?"

"Two, but they're home."

"Stand up."

Kirby's eyes opened, incredulous at first then quickly flaring as his mouth flattened.

"Don't be so touchy," Bacon said, evaluating the reaction. "You were a cop long enough to know the routine."

Kirby rose, his mouth still tight. He straightened the jacket of his pin-striped gray suit, which was a little wide in the shoulders but of excellent material. Keogh, at a glance from Bacon, made a perfunctory inspection and stepped back.

"Is that your desk?" Bacon said, indicating the one on the left. He nodded again to Keogh and the sergeant went over to examine the drawers.

Kirby sat down. He was still sore but he made a suggestion. "It looks like Tom's gun," he said. "You could check it with his permit."

"Did he carry it much?"

"No."

"Where'd he keep it?"

"In his desk. In the drawer that's been pulled out."

The photographer turned out his lights and Bacon asked the precinct lieutenant if he would empty Brady's pockets. When this was done he asked Keogh to see if the ambulance men were ready. They came in a minute later and now Murdock, who had been staring straight ahead, took out a cigarette and deliberately fixed his glance at the window.

In spite of his attempt to concentrate he could see the movement from the corner of one eye and when the stretcher began to move his throat was hard and there was a stinging at the back of his eyeballs. Only when the door had closed would he look at Bacon, listening again, speculating when he could, his deep-seated anger still seething.

Bacon was looking through Brady's wallet now and presently he asked the fingerprint man if he could read the number on the revolver without messing it up.

"I never got a decent print from a gun yet," the man said, "but you never can tell."

He bent over with a flashlight and poked at the revolver with the tip of a pencil. When he read off a number Bacon said:

"It's his, all right." He glanced at Kirby. "So how does he get shot with his own gun?"

"You just asking," Kirby said, "or am I supposed to guess?"

"Let's all guess," Bacon said.

"Whoever it was must have had a gun of his own."

"If he pulled it," Bacon said, "Brady might have sneaked that drawer open."

"He would have tried," Kirby said. "He wasn't the kind to sit still on a thing like that."

Bacon nodded thoughtfully in agreement. "He gets it out but the other guy spots it in time. Still covering Brady, he makes him put it on the desk. He picks it up and now Brady must think the guy's going to use it. If there's powder marks on his shirt it must mean he tried to lunge for the gun and didn't quite make it."

He swore softly, a frustrated and bitter sound; then, checking himself, his manner became deliberately businesslike.

"We'd better inventory the desk," he said. "Especially that drawer that's pulled out. . . . Is that a typewriter ribbon?" he asked, pointing at the overturned wastebasket. "Did he do his own typing?" he said to Kirby.

"He typed his reports first and then had them copied."

Bacon studied the portable typewriter on the desk and told the fingerprint man to put it in its case and take it along.

"If it's a new ribbon," he said, "maybe it'll have some writing on it you can read. . . . Now what about that filing cabinet, Frank?"

"He kept the carbons of his reports in it."

"How many? What I mean is, how full was the drawer? How much room did the carbons take up?"

"I don't know exactly."

"Give me an idea."

"About like that," Kirby said, and held his hands a foot or more apart.

"Too much to carry in your pockets or in your arms?"

"If they were tied up you could carry them under your arm." Kirby stood up and went over to the desk. "He had a briefcase," he said, and after looking about went into the partitioned office. "Unless he had it at home that must be it," he said finally.

"He had it with him this afternoon," Murdock said.

Bacon turned, brows bunched over his gray eyes. "How do you know?"

"He was at the studio."

"When?"

Murdock told him and Bacon turned to Kirby. "Did you know that?"

"Sure. I phoned him there to tell him about the Kelleher thing. He came back here and we talked it over and decided how to work on it."

"Did he have the briefcase then?"

"Yes, now that I stop to think of it."

"What did he want with you?" Bacon said to Murdock.

"He had some things he wanted photographed. He wanted me to make some negatives."

"What sort of things?"

"Well—some affidavits, copies of this and that, a couple of birth certificates."

"What were they about?"

"I don't know."

"You must have some idea," Bacon said with mounting impatience.

Murdock replied in level tones, explaining Brady's attitude and what he had said. "I didn't read much and what I saw didn't make much sense to me."

"Maybe you'll remember some of them later," Bacon said dryly.

"Maybe."

"Okay. Start thinking. . . . What was he working on?" he said to Kirby.

"He's been out of town for a month," Kirby said. "Just got back last night." He went on to say that he had taken over Brady's bread-and-butter accounts—a couple of weekly payroll jobs, occasional work for the Northeast Insurance Company checking job applicants, some security work for a food chain.

"He was away a month?" Bacon said with some surprise. "On one job? It must have been important."

He paused, and when Kirby offered no comment he said: "Do you know who he was working for?"

"I think it was the Alderson family."

"The Beacon Street Aldersons?" Bacon's eyes opened and he whistled softly. "I'll be damned," he said. "I wouldn't think they'd let a detective in the door." Then, as a new thought came to him, he turned back to Murdock. "What happened to the films?"

Murdock explained what he had done and Bacon said: "Did Brady pick them up?"

"He must have," Murdock said. "They weren't in my desk at eight o'clock."

"What did he do with the original stuff?"

"He tucked it in a manila envelope and put it in his pocket."

Bacon looked around, speaking to his men but addressing no one. "No envelope?" he said. "No negatives?" He took a breath and swore again. "No reports either, not even the briefcase." He might have said more if a detective had not opened the door to say that a Mr. Enders wanted to see him.

"Enders?" Bacon said, frowning again. "Is that the lawyer—never mind, ask him to come in."

Arthur Enders was a graying, handsome man of forty-five or so with a lithe, muscular figure and the sort of face that is copied by advertisers who need someone with a sportsman's look to endorse their products. He had a resonant voice and a gracious, assured manner that managed to suggest somehow that he had been born for the better things of life. Now, unbelting his trench coat and shaking the rain from his hat, he glanced about, nodded to Murdock and then concentrated on Bacon.

"You wanted to see me, Mr. Enders?" the lieutenant said.

"Not exactly," Enders said. "I came to see Mr. Brady—"

"Why?"

"I had an appointment. Someone downstairs told me what had happened. They said you were in charge so I thought I'd better come up."

"Oh," Bacon said. "Well, when did you see Brady last?"

"About a month ago."

"Then you made this appointment by telephone?"

"He called late this afternoon and said he'd like to talk to me for a few minutes. He asked if I could stop by around nine thirty"—he paused to glance at his wrist watch—"and I said I could. I see I'm a little late."

"He didn't say why he wanted to see you? . . . You knew he was working for the Alderson family," he said when Enders shook his head.

"I knew that, yes, but I don't know why or what he had been doing."

"Who hired him?"

"Mrs. Alderson—that's Mrs. Harriett Alderson."

"But she didn't tell you why?"

"No."

"You're the family attorney. Yet you made no attempt—"

Enders smiled faintly. "If you knew Mrs. Alderson you'd know that once she made up her mind—"

"She didn't confide in you?"

"Not in this case."

"Just how did she go about hiring a detective anyway?"

"She talked to me first, after she'd made up her mind. I tried to find out why she wanted one and when that was no good I tried to discourage her. When I saw I was wasting my time I suggested Mr. Brady because I knew his reputation. I think she checked with Murdock," he said, and glanced round for confirmation.

Murdock corroborated the statement and repeated what he had told Tom Brady that afternoon.

"She didn't tell you why she wanted a detective either?" Bacon chewed on the denial a moment, a look of aggravation in his eyes. Apparently realizing he was getting nowhere in his present line of questioning, he took another tack and looked at Kirby.

"Tom typed his own reports," he said, "and someone copied them."

"That's right," Kirby said. "His typing was pretty rough."

"Who did the copying?"

"A girl by the name of Sally Fisher. She works at the *Courier*."

"She's on the society staff," Murdock said. "She lives in the same building as Tom. She used to copy his stuff—he didn't have too much—at night."

"What's the address?"

Murdock gave it and Sergeant Keogh wrote it down. "Maybe she can help us," Bacon said, "but first I think we'd better have a talk with Mrs. Alderson." He nodded at Keogh and the two moved to the doorway where Bacon gave some low-voiced instructions before Keogh went out. Now coming back to Enders, he said:

"Do you want to call her and tell her we're coming?"

"Not particularly."

Bacon reddened slightly but ignored the remark. "Brady's been working a month for Mrs. Alderson," he said grimly. "That suggests that she was willing to spend quite a lot of money. Someone walked in here tonight and killed him, apparently before he'd had a chance to hand in his reports. They're gone. So are the affidavits and material he spent a month getting, plus some films he had made this afternoon."

He took a breath and said, still grim: "Tom Brady was a cop who had the liking and respect of anyone who ever knew or worked with him. In my book, he's still a cop, and that means all of us in the department are going to give this investigation a little extra something, Mr. Enders. We're going to nail this killer and if it happens to be someone named Alderson it'll be just too bad."

He continued quickly as Enders seemed about to protest. "You're the family lawyer," he said. "Okay, we'll take you along with us and you can protect their rights. So suppose you telephone Mrs. Alderson and tell her what happened. You can say that I suggest that she have the other members of the family on hand if she can locate them. And tell her this, Mr. Enders. Tell her that if she doesn't want to talk to me tonight, I'll have the whole crowd subpoena'd and they can come down to the D.A.'s office in the morning and we'll make it official."

That was quite a speech for Bacon, and to Murdock there was no bluff in what he had to say. He meant every word and Arthur Enders apparently got the same impression. He sighed audibly, shrugged, and went over to the telephone. As he dialed, Bacon went into a huddle with the precinct lieutenant and the other detectives.

Murdock paid no attention to what Enders said but stood up to get his coat. He put Kirby's hat aside and now Kirby came over and put it on. He took the folded coat that Murdock gave him and hung it over his arm and by the time Murdock had slipped into his own dampened coat Enders had finished his phone call.

"Did she give you an argument?" Bacon asked.

"I told her what you said," Enders said dryly. "Maybe that convinced her."

Bacon nodded and came over to Murdock. "Where're you going?"

Until that moment Murdock had not thought about it. He had been thinking about Tom Brady and worrying about his own helplessness and mentally abusing himself for not reading the documents he had photographed when he had the chance. For it seemed to him now that Bacon was on the right track, that somehow the things that Brady had learned were responsible for his death.

"I don't know," he said. "Maybe I'll go with you."

"That's what I had in mind," Bacon said. "You're a friend of the family; you can front for me. . . . You too, Kirby," he said. "We'll ride together and Murdock can keep thinking about those documents he photographed. . . . You can follow along in your car, Mr. Enders," he said. "And Sergeant Keogh can follow you."

6

AS IT turned out, the company car had been left for Murdock and so he put his camera and case in the back and the three of them sat in front, Bacon in the middle. The rain had moderated to a drizzle now but Murdock took it easy and presently Kirby cleared his throat.

"I've been thinking, Lieutenant," he said. "Maybe I've got something that will help. It's about Enders."

"Ahh—what about him?"

"I got a long distance call from Tom about a week or so

after he left. From San Francisco. He said he had a couple of jobs I might be able to handle for him. He said I'd be working for him and he'd pay me but that he would get it from Aldersons in the end. He wanted me to check on Enders."

Bacon said: "Ahh—" again, a new interest in his tone. "You mean tail him?"

"Not tail him," Kirby said. "Brady wanted to know about his finances and how his credit was—things like that. He said I should snoop around and see what I could find."

"So?"

"Enders owes dough. His stock market account is margined to the limit and he's got a couple of good-sized notes at the bank. There's a plaster on that forty-five-foot cruiser he's got at Hingham and a plaster on the summer place down there."

"Well, well," said Bacon. "You never know, do you?"

"He's payin' alimony to two wives," Kirby continued, "but he's still living it up and taking trips to Florida and Bermuda. Where do you think he got that tan so early in the season?"

He said other things but Murdock no longer heard them. Enders's activities and expenses did not surprise him, but it had never occurred to him that the man's credit could be so extended. For Enders & Enders was a law firm of distinction and long standing that had been started by Arthur's grandfather. Now there was only Arthur and a couple of young junior partners and the business currently dealt less with the law, as such, than with the management of certain estates, the most important being the Aldersons'.

Murdock knew that the account had been inherited from Arthur's father, who had been a life-long friend of the late Edward Alderson. What Arthur had done to preserve or increase the estate was something about which Murdock had no idea. He did know that Enders also had the Alderson Tool Company as an account and that he had been appointed administrator of George Alderson's estate when George had been killed in the automobile crash and died intestate. So far as Murdock knew, the estate was still in some stage of probate. . . .

"Okay," Bacon was saying. "Now did you tell Brady what you found out?"

"This morning," Kirby said. "I think maybe that's why Tom called Enders this afternoon, but that's only a guess."

Bacon said: "Hmm," and considered the information a bit longer and then he said: "You said Tom wanted you to do a couple of things for him. What was the other?"

"To check a guy named Barry Denham. He's Mrs. George Alderson's brother. Came to town a couple of months ago and is staying at the Clay Hotel."

Murdock could have made a slight correction here—he knew Denham was not a full brother but only a half brother to Rita—but he let Kirby go on, remembering that he had met Denham once. According to Rita, Denham was an actor who had recently been in Mexico and had come to Boston hoping to get a job at one of the summer theaters either in Maine or on the Cape.

"Denham, hunh?" Bacon said, as though searching his memory in some effort to place the name. "What's he do?"

"Nothing."

"Has he got dough?"

"He's got enough to sleep late in the morning and go to the track every afternoon. Nights he hangs around here and there tanking up a bit. He takes in the fights when he can but he spends most of his time at the Club Saville. He's got a girl there in the chorus line."

"What else?"

"That's about it."

"Does he see much of his sister?"

"She's been to see him at the Clay a couple of times since I've been watching him. They've had dinner twice." He hesitated, his tone speculative as he continued. "Also I think somebody else is interested enough in Denham to check on him now and then."

"Yeah? Who?"

"Jerry Alderson."

Bacon repeated the name and then he nudged Murdock. "I'm getting a little confused with all these Aldersons. Set them up for me. Who's Harriett?"

"She's the mother," Murdock said. "The one that rules the roost."

"The one that hired Brady."

"Right. A widow who had three sons. Donald is the oldest. He married a Virginia girl named Gloria Starrett about four years ago. George, the middle brother, was the one who was killed in that accident. He married a girl named Rita Carr."

"This is Denham's sister? With that name?"

"Half sister."

"Okay."

"Jerry's the youngest son. He's a partner in an advertising agency here in town."

"And you say you think he's been checking on Denham?" Bacon said to Kirby. "Why would that be?"

"I don't know unless maybe he's sort of stuck on his brother's widow. I caught him watching the Clay on two different times when she was with Denham."

Bacon nudged Murdock again. "Let's try the Clay first," he said. "Let's see if Denham's around."

Murdock did as directed, and a minute or so later he pulled into the No Parking space in front of the entrance. As Bacon got out and told him to wait he glanced round to find Arthur Enders's foreign-made convertible behind him and a police car with Keogh at the wheel bringing up the rear. By the time he had a cigarette going, Bacon was back.

"Not in," he said. "Let's roll."

The Alderson town house was on the river side of Beacon Street, a four-story brick-and-stone structure that had a little more frontage than some. A car was pulling into the only available parking space in front of the building as Murdock approached, and as he slowed down he saw Jerry Alderson cross the sidewalk. He told Bacon about it as he eased on for another hundred feet and found a place of his own.

Beacon was a one-way street here, and as they got out of the car Murdock noticed that Enders and Keogh had found parking places across the way and now they stood in front of the house until the two had joined them. Bacon told Keogh to wait in the car and let his office know where he would be; then he nodded to Enders.

Originally the house had been designed with high stone steps which led to what was now the second floor; in re-modeling, the basement became the first floor and was entered by a sidewalk-level door which had been recessed slightly into the façade. The man who opened this door wore an alpaca coat and had more hair in his eyebrows than he had on his head. He was of indeterminate age, his shoulders stooped but powerful looking, his voice soft and unaccented. His name was Henderson.

Enders carried the ball until they were in an oblong

foyer, where Henderson took their coats and hats. A tiny
elevator for Harriett Alderson's use had been added in recent years and its shaft jutted from the right wall. A wide
and carpeted stairway mounted from the left and when
Henderson said that they were expected, Enders led the
way to the second-floor drawing room at the rear and overlooking the river.

The Alderson family waited for them at the far end of
the room and watched them enter in silence: Harriett in
a wing chair in the center of the irregular semi-circle, as
befitted her authority, Donald and his wife Gloria on the
divan to the left, Jerry and Rita in two upholstered chairs
at the right. There was an empty chair on Harriett's immediate right and when Enders had made the introduc-
tions a wave of her hand indicated that he was to sit beside
her. Murdock and Kirby were left to seat themselves
wherever they could and Bacon remained standing.

When he had cleared his throat he said he appreciated
their co-operation, and as he went on with his preliminary
remarks Murdock mentally called the roll, starting with
Harriett Alderson, who sat erect in her chair, a shawl over
her knees and a cane at her side.

A slender, striking-looking woman in her early sixties,
with more gray hair than black, she had a thin, high-
bridged nose that gave her a proud and haughty look and
now there was a tightness at the corners of her mouth, as
though put there by a disapproving mind. In her younger
days she had been well known in society circles as a horse-
woman and she had continued to ride until a few years
previous when her horse had refused a jump and thrown
her into a fence, breaking a hip and smashing a knee. The
hip had mended but the knee had not. More recently an
arthritic condition had set in so that she could move only

with the help of her cane, but because she was a strong-willed and perhaps resentful woman, she continued out-wardly to deny the existence of pain or any weakness of the flesh.

Murdock's glance moved on to Donald Alderson, who was at forty a tall, lean, and somehow ascetic-looking man with a small but ingrown frown that may have come from a preoccupied air put there by his duties as manager of the family business. In contrast, his wife Gloria was an auburn-haired and green-eyed woman eight years his junior, with a tall, full-bodied figure that was not yet fat.

He glanced at the blonde Rita and remembered their conversation that afternoon; he looked at Jerry, who was the rebel of the family. And now he remembered George, who had been the solid man of the three brothers, and it came to him again how much he missed him. For they had been classmates in college and he had been an usher at the wedding and it was only through George that he had come to know something about the rest of the family. . . . Deliberately now he brought his mind back to the moment and tried not to think of George or of Tom Brady.

"I'm sorry to hear about Mr. Brady," Harriett was saying. "But I fail to see just why you should think we can help you."

"He worked for you, Mrs. Alderson," Bacon said, being very patient. "I understand he was at it for a month, travel-ing all over the country. If we knew what he was trying to do it might give us a lead. . . . What was the nature of this job? What was he—or you—trying to prove?"

The woman looked at Enders. "Do I have to answer that, Arthur?"

"Certainly not," Enders said.

She nodded with approval, as though she had known what the answer would be.

"It was a personal matter, Lieutenant. A family matter if you like. You might even call it a whim of mine. It was definitely not anything that would have interested the police or I would have gone to them in the first place."

Bacon's lips tightened slightly but his tone remained patient.

"From what I've heard it looks as if Brady's trip was successful. He said something to Mr. Murdock about a bonus."

"There would have been a bonus under the proper circumstances."

"Have you seen his reports?"

"No."

"Was he in touch with you today?"

"By telephone. He said he would bring me a full report in the morning. He said he wanted a permanent record of certain documents, though I'm not quite sure what he meant."

"Whoever killed him cleaned out his files, Mrs. Alderson," Bacon said. "There are no reports that we've been able to find. There are no documents, nor any permanent records of them. We think he was killed because of the work he had done, or what he knew. If so the assumption has to be made that one of you may be involved."

"What rot," Harriett said stonily. "If you're suggesting that anyone here could be guilty of—"

"I said involved," Bacon cut in. "Not guilty."

"Don't quibble, Lieutenant!"

That one brought a slight flush to Bacon's neck but it did not influence his thinking. Realizing that he had reached a temporary impasse, he quickly took another tack.

"Were you home all evening, Mrs. Alderson?"

"All day, Lieutenant."

"You were here for dinner then. With whom?" said Bacon, minding his grammar.

Harriett's dark direct gaze remained steady but a corner of her mouth twitched in what might have been a smile.

"What you want from us is alibis, is that it? . . . Is that the proper term, Arthur?" she said to Enders. "I'm not sure I like it," she added to Bacon.

"Nor do I," said Bacon, and now his tone was more blunt. "Maybe I'd better start all over again," he said. "A man was killed tonight. He happened to be a friend of mine, a friend of Mr. Murdock's. Even if he wasn't it would be my job—along with a lot of other officers—to find out who killed him. We intend to do just that, Mrs. Alderson, with your co-operation or without it."

He looked at Enders, his tone still stiff. "Do you want to remind these people again that this is a murder investigation? I don't seem to be getting through."

"I'm not sure I care for that sort of insolence, Arthur," Harriett said.

Enders looked uncomfortable, but before he could make any reply Bacon continued.

"All right, Mrs. Alderson," he said. "You can suit yourself. You are going to be investigated—all of you; make no mistake about that. That investigation will be continued until you are cleared of suspicion, and you can start now or you can go down to the District Attorney's office in the morning and answer—or not answer—his questions officially. I came here because I thought it would be easier—"

The woman waved him to silence with an imperious gesture, but what she said indicated that Bacon had scored a point or two.

"Spare me the details, please. Get on with it. . . . I had dinner here tonight with Donald and Rita."

"Thank you," Bacon said, and turned to Donald Alderson.

Murdock watched as Bacon phrased his questions and it occurred to him that Donald's voice fitted him exactly. In his neat, dark suit and thin-rimmed glasses, with his thinning sandy hair and high forehead and his mother's high-bridged nose, he spoke in precise accents as he explained how he had gone to his office after dinner.

"That would be the Alderson Tool Company," Bacon said. "In Somerville? And what time was that?"

"I left here about eight, I think. I came back about fifteen minutes before you arrived."

Bacon made some notes and turned to Rita. She glanced at Murdock once as Bacon spoke and that was long enough for Murdock to recall the startling dark-blue eyes, to remember what Kirby had said about her half brother. Except for an occasional glance at Jerry Alderson she had been watching Bacon, and her young face seemed paler now, but composed; her chin was up as she said she left the house about eight thirty.

"I wanted to walk," she said. "I wanted some fresh air."

"In the rain?"

"It wasn't raining then," she said. "I got caught in it before I got back but—"

"Did you walk any place in particular?"

"No. Just—down Beacon, and along the Avenue to Boylston and then back."

"And how long did that take?"

"Ohh"—she hesitated and glanced at her mother-in-law —"I guess three-quarters of an hour."

Bacon nodded and added to his notes. "What about you, Mrs. Alderson?" he said, and glanced at Gloria. "You were out for dinner?"

To Murdock it seemed that there was a slight hesitation in her reply. She was wearing a tailored suit of some dark-green material that looked custom-made, and her full red mouth, which contrasted so sharply with her clear white skin, moved once before she said:

"At the Ritz."

"Alone?"

Again the hesitation and this time her green eyes started to move sideways before she pulled them back.

"Yes." She straightened slightly as though she had just made up her mind about something and said: "If you want to know the truth, Lieutenant, I was in rather a foul mood. My husband and I had—well, you could call it a disagreement, and I decided it might be better if I ate alone."

Murdock eyed Bacon, wondering if he would accept a story which to him seemed unconvincing. When the lieutenant gave his attention to Jerry Alderson, Murdock listened while the pattern was repeated.

At the moment, Jerry seemed less concerned than some of the others. He was, Murdock knew, the extrovert of the family, a good-looking fellow with close-cropped curly hair, a determined jaw, and a mouth that was normally quick to smile. He had always been popular, not only with men but with women, and though he seldom made his social rounds without an escort, he was, at thirty, still a bachelor and a desirable one from nearly every viewpoint. As such he was subject to certain pressures for which he had a good-natured but stock explanation, a sort of run-

ning gag that, while basically true, was seldom believed.
He simply said that to marry without his mother's permission would mean being disinherited and that he had not
yet won approval for any of his girl friends.

As these thoughts came to Murdock he glanced again at
Rita, for he had noticed that Jerry had looked her way
several times during the past few minutes. Each time their
eyes had met there had come from Jerry a veiled but noticeable smile that seemed to speak of some secret understanding that had nothing to do with what was taking
place in the room. To Murdock it seemed like the sort of
look people in love exchanged and he paid attention now
as Jerry explained how he had worked at his office until
some time after six. He named a restaurant where he had
dined with a client.

"He left at eight thirty," he said, "and I went back to
the office for about a half hour, though I wouldn't swear
to the time. I do know that at nine fifteen I was having a
drink at the Club Saville bar."

"Thanks," Bacon said. "Thanks very much." Then, in the
same tone and without hesitation, he added: "That leaves
you, Mr. Enders. . . . If you don't mind."

Enders seemed ready for the question and his handsome
face warped in a small but tolerant grin as he told how
he had worked until after seven before going out to dinner.

"And where was that?"

Still showing no embarrassment, Enders shook his head.
"Suppose we skip that one for now, Lieutenant."

"If you say so," Bacon said, his glance narrowing
slightly. "Alone?" he said. "Or do we skip that too?"

"For now."

"Where were you at eight thirty?"

"Driving out to Brookline to see a business associate."

"Did you see him?"

"He wasn't home, so I came back to the office. Then I remembered I had a date with Brady."

He stood up as he finished, his smile still there, his manner gracious. He took time to glance slowly round the room as though he wanted to make sure that no one had been overlooked, making a slight bow as he came to Harriett Alderson.

"I'm sure the lieutenant appreciates your co-operation," he said in resonant tones. "Actually it wasn't too much of an ordeal, was it?"

The woman liked that. She smiled at her attorney and then at Bacon and by now Bacon had had it and he knew it. He snapped his notebook shut and tightened his mouth while the flush crept slowly up from his neck to his cheeks. He mumbled something about keeping in touch with them, thanked them, and turned on his heel.

Frank Kirby, who had not opened his mouth since he had been introduced, looked at Murdock and shrugged. They went out of the room, Bacon leading the way, and as they came to the landing a telephone rang somewhere below them. By the time they had reached the foyer Henderson was holding a telephone towards Bacon.

"Your office, I believe, sir," he said, and then turned to get their coats and hats.

Bacon said: "Yeah. Yeah. . . . Right. . . . We'll get over there."

Murdock hung his coat over his arm and so did Kirby; Bacon put his on and centered his hat. They went out into the night that was clearing and warmer.

"The Fisher girl," Bacon said. "The one that did the copying for Brady."

"Sally Fisher," Murdock said, the pressure of some quick alarm accenting his words. "What about her?"

"A couple of guys jumped her as she came into her building. Grabbed her bag and knocked her down. It could be just a mugging by a couple of neighborhood punks but she's all right now. There's somebody with her, so we'll stop at the Clay before we talk to her."

7

WHILE Lieutenant Bacon signaled across the street to Sergeant Keogh, Murdock threw his coat on the shelf behind the back seat to get it out of the way and then slid in behind the wheel. With Bacon once more beside him, Kirby closed the door and Murdock pulled out into the one-way traffic, watching his rearview mirror to see that Keogh was following. When he could he turned left, made another left at Boylston, and five minutes later he was back in front of the Clay Hotel, an ancient structure whose walls had been sandblasted to give it some semblance of modernity and whose original charm had been scarred by attempts at remodeling to get a bigger bar and restaurant trade.

This time Bacon indicated that Murdock and Kirby could accompany him and so they went into the lobby and started for the desk. Halfway there, Murdock glanced about and spotted Barry Denham reading a bulldog edition of the *Courier,* so he hurried ahead and took the lieutenant's arm.

"I think that's Denham over in the corner," he said, and pointed.

"Good," Bacon said. "You can introduce me."

Denham apparently saw them coming, for he put down the paper and then, recognizing Murdock, he smiled and stood up. "Hi, Murdock," he said. "Want to see me?"

"We were going to ask for you at the desk but I happened to see you sitting here. This is Lieutenant Bacon and Frank Kirby—Barry Denham."

They all said hello without attempting to shake hands and Denham, looking at Bacon, said: "Town cop?"

"Homicide," Bacon said.

"Good," Denham said, and grinned. "That puts me in the clear. What's on your mind?"

"Like to ask you some questions."

"Shoot."

"Mind telling us what you've been doing tonight?"

"Since when?"

"Oh—say five o'clock."

"I was at the track this afternoon," Denham said. "I got here about six and tossed off a couple and had a shower and a nap. I didn't go out until about nine o'clock."

"Was it raining then?"

Denham hesitated and pursed his lips, a big man, well built but soft looking, with dark, wavy hair worn too long for Murdock's taste, and a small trim mustache. His eyes were small and light blue, the color all the more noticeable when contrasted to his dark brows and skin. He had a certain superficial handsomeness in spite of the heavy face and small mouth, but seen close like this it came to Murdock that here was a man he would never entirely trust. He had an idea that Denham was the sort who could lie convincingly without giving the matter a second thought;

he also had the impression that when crossed the man could be both truculent and mean. Now, tipping his head to one side, Denham said:

"It was just starting."

"Then what?"

"I went over to the Saville and had dinner. . . . So what's the beef, Lieutenant? Who got killed?"

Bacon told him and Denham said he'd never heard of Tom Brady. Bacon said Brady was working for the Aldersons, that he had just come from there.

"Have you got some identification, Denham?" he said abruptly.

Just as abruptly, Denham's pale eyes narrowed and his mustache flattened with some movement of his mouth.

"Why don't you buzz off?" he said nastily. "I answered your questions about tonight. If they don't check out, come back again."

Bacon didn't raise his voice but the cadence changed. Murdock, watching him and knowing how he worked, found a certain satisfaction in the way he handled Denham's bluff. With no variation in his expression he said:

"Do you wear a coat, Denham?"

"Yeah. Right there." And he pointed to the raincoat that had been tossed across an adjoining chair.

"Put it on," Bacon said. "Or carry it if you like. . . . Let's go down to Headquarters."

"What could you book me on if I did?"

"From what I hear about you vagrancy would stick. Come on."

He reached for Denham and the big man pulled back and suddenly his defiance was gone. He made a half-hearted attempt to smile and his glance dropped as he pulled out his wallet.

"Identification?" he said. "Sure. You don't have to get tough about it. Here, help yourself."

"You take it out," Bacon said. "Whatever you got there."

Denham extracted what looked to Murdock like a driver's license and a social security card. Bacon looked them over, then returned them.

"I hear you're an actor," he said. "Working yet?"

"No, but I've got some lines out for the summer."

"You're Rita Alderson's half brother?"

"That's right."

"She been supporting you?"

"I'm on an allowance. A grand a week."

"How long you been in town?" Bacon said, ignoring the sarcasm.

"About two months."

"Do you know the Aldersons?"

"Slightly. I was there for dinner once." Denham's smile was easy again. "I don't think the old girl liked me. I haven't been back."

"All right, Denham," Bacon said. "Stick around. We may want a statement tomorrow."

He turned then, and with a slight nod to Murdock, started for the door, his back straight, his hat centered, and the tails of his raincoat flapping at his calves.

Sally Fisher lived in an old brownstone not far from Hemenway Street. Like many of its neighbors it had been converted to small apartments but the high steps were still there, as was the entryway that was seldom closed except in winter. A detective was waiting here when Bacon led the way up the steps and from what he said it was apparent that he had been sent by Bacon to make a search of Tom Brady's apartment, which was on the second floor.

From Bacon's point of view the results had been negligible.

"There was no gun," the detective said. "No reports of any kind that I could find. There's a fireplace that works and it had some paper ashes in it but that's all. . . . Here's a spare key I got from the landlord," he said, "in case you want to look."

Bacon said all right. He dismissed the man, and they went inside and up the worn stairway, past the door on the second floor that Murdock had visited so often in recent years and now, as they climbed the last flight, he felt again the depression and the wrench of his emotions as he recalled the weekly game of pinochle and the beer and the conversation that had become something of a ritual for both of them. The thought stayed with him as Bacon knocked at the door of the top apartment and only when a detective opened it and he saw Sally Fisher was he able to put aside the memory.

She sat on a studio couch which faced the door, a small and neatly rounded girl, with hazel eyes and chestnut hair cut in a short, close-fitting bob. She had a tilted nose and a cute mouth that could dissolve into a sparkling smile, and because she was so often smiling it shocked him to see the tear-stained cheeks and watch the eyes fill again when she saw him.

"Hey," he said thickly, and went over to sit beside her, taking a soft, damp hand in his and squeezing it. "You're all right, aren't you?"

She nodded and made a small hiccuping sound as she tried to swallow.

"I'm not crying about that," she said forlornly. "It—it's about Mr. Brady."

"Yeah," said Murdock, and now he could do nothing more to help her.

"Why?" she asked in her distress. "How could anyone do a thing like that? . . . He was such a nice man," she said, and now her face crumpled again and she was crying openly.

Murdock held on to her hand but his face was hot. Angry glints showed in his dark eyes as he tried to concentrate on what the detective was saying to Bacon.

He understood at once that this was a precinct man who had nothing to do with the murder but had been sent from the station house when Sally had telephoned to report what had happened to her. From what the detective said now it appeared that Sally had had an early dinner with a girl friend and then gone to an early movie. She had come home about nine thirty and it was when she stepped into the vestibule that the two men, asking only if her name was Sally Fisher, grabbed her, knocking her down when she struggled and taking her handbag. She had come up-stairs to find the lock had been forced, but it was not until after she had called the police that she realized her apart-ment had already been searched.

Now Bacon came over to stand in front of her, hat in hand and his voice surprisingly gentle.

"I know this isn't going to be easy, Miss Fisher," he said. "I know how you feel about Tom Brady; we all feel the same way. But we're going to need your help. Try to tell me again just what you told the detective. . . . That's the girl," he said, when she lifted her chin and wiped her eyes.

No one interrupted as she spoke and it was not until she finished that Bacon asked if anything in the apartment was missing.

"No," she said. "That's the funny part."

"Was there anything in your bag except personal things?"

"Nothing. Not even much money."

Bacon paused reflectively and Murdock asked the question that was uppermost in his mind.

"Did Tom call you this afternoon?" he asked. "Did he ask you to stop in the studio and get an envelope from my desk?"

"Why, no," she said, her eyes opening wide. "He didn't."

"But you copied his reports," Bacon said.

"Evenings. There weren't too many."

"You knew he'd come back from his trip?"

"Yes. He stopped in to see me last night."

"Did he have a lot of things for you to copy?"

"No." She paused when she saw Bacon's expression; then said: "Oh, I know what you mean. But you see what he did on his trip was to mail me these rough reports each week. He'd type them out and send them to me so I wouldn't have so much to do all at once."

"Ahh," said Bacon with some relief. "Now can you tell me what those reports were about?"

"Well—not very well. I mean—"

"But you read them when you typed them."

"In a way, yes. But you can copy things, once you get used to it, without hardly knowing what you're copying. You can even be thinking about something else. It's sort of—I don't know—automatic, I guess. And besides, this was different."

"Oh?" said Bacon, still unconvinced. "How?"

She thought a moment, head tilting and her brows bunched. "Well, maybe it sounds sort of silly now, but it was sort of like we were playing a game. I mean, when he first asked me if I would help him out he explained that as a private detective his work had to be confidential between him and his client. He said it was sort of privileged, like a lawyer and his client, or a doctor."

Bacon grunted softly to show his disapproval of Brady's opinion but he did not interrupt.

"I knew what he meant and I guess I exaggerated things when I talked to him. He used to laugh, but I think it was fun for him too when I pretended that he was a very important detective and that each report was especially hush-hush or secretly dangerous. I really think he meant it at first when he said it would be best if I didn't know what I was copying, but the way we played it he would bring a new report and I'd say, is this about the hydrogen bomb and he'd say no, it was the case history of a suspected spy —or something like that.

"But I did read one or two at first," she confessed, her glance dropping. "Until I found out they weren't very exciting. Mostly there wasn't anything but times and places that some man had been. They were really pretty dull when you didn't know the people."

Murdock understood her explanation because he knew Brady. Talking to Sally like that, playing the game with her, was the sort of thing he would do. Bacon seemed to accept the story too, and though he sighed heavily he was not yet ready to admit defeat.

"All right," he said. "But what happened to the roughs he mailed in?"

"Oh, he took everything last night. He always took his roughs. He said it was important to destroy them so they'd never be around to embarrass anyone."

Bacon massaged his chin and for a moment his gray eyes held a baffled look; then he swallowed and said: "You want to help, don't you?"

"Oh, yes, I do."

"Then maybe if you had some time, and tried real hard, you might remember something about those reports. Not what they meant so much as maybe some details, or names or places or certain statements Brady may have made. You don't have to worry about whether they're important or not, or even if they make sense. Just jot down anything that you can remember. Will you try?"

She frowned but nodded. "Yes. Of course I will."

"Is there a back door?"

"Through there," she said, pointing.

Bacon told the detective to see if the door was locked and the man said he had already looked and it was. Bacon went over to examine the chain lock on the hall door.

"Just slip this on when we leave," he said to the girl. "I don't think you'll have any more trouble tonight. If you're sure you're all right, we'll go along."

"Yes," she said, coming to her feet. "I'm quite all right now. And I will try to remember; I promise."

Bacon said that would be fine and then, nodding to the others, led the way from the room, stopping after the door had closed to wait until he heard the chain lock slip into place.

Down on the sidewalk Bacon asked Murdock where he was going from here and Murdock said: "Back to the office." Bacon told him to keep thinking and then asked Kirby if he could drop him anywhere. Kirby said yes, and as they started for the police car Murdock slid into the sedan and snapped on the two radios. When the tubes had warmed he called the office and said there was nothing new on the Brady case; he said he was bringing the car in.

A light was burning in T. A. Wyman's office when Murdock walked through the city room at twenty minutes of twelve, so he knocked once and opened the door far enough to stick his head inside.

"Come in." Wyman took the cigar from his mouth and pointed it at a chair. "Sit down."

Murdock accepted the invitation gratefully, his weariness making itself felt as he leaned back and stretched his legs out. For silent seconds he surveyed the wing tips of his Oxfords and noted the damage done by the rain. When he had made a mental reservation to get a shine the first thing in the morning he said, not looking up:

"What do you hear about Walt Carey?"

"The latest is that he's going to be okay," Wyman said. "No brain damage but it may be a while before anyone can talk to him."

He waited for some reply and when none came he eased back in the chair, puffed gently on his cigar, and let the silence build. It was not often that Murdock came to his office and when he did it was never just to pass the time of day. He was not sure what was bothering Murdock at the moment but he was willing to wait, and as he did so it came to him again that he was lucky to have a man like Murdock on his staff.

It was not just a matter of experience and training and intelligence; it was something more, a quality hard to define and made up of many things, but peculiarly Murdock's. Not just his appearance, which was in his favor, not the casual way he wore his clothes—they were conservative, well tailored and in excellent taste—nor the way he carried himself.

Part of his value to the paper could be attributed to his ability to get pictures often denied to others and his willingness, when necessary, to crash through a crowd with camera and equipment case. Perhaps a more important part was due to the fact that people liked him; for in people his taste was catholic and he could talk as easily to a truck driver or a circulation hustler as he could to the mother of the bride. His manner was easily adjustable to the circumstances and although he could be tough when he had to, it was a facet of his character that seldom showed; it was only when his own self-integrity or some question of principle was involved that the hard and uncompromising side of his nature became evident.

Wyman had never told him any of this, because Wyman was a businessman and he had a budget to think of. Except for a couple of editors, and a columnist who was more popular than outstanding, Murdock got as much money as anyone in the shop and Wyman wanted to keep it that way. Now, not knowing what was bothering Murdock but certain that it would presently be told, he was willing to wait.

The request, when it came, was both simple and surprising. Without changing his position, his dark gaze somber and morose as it came up to meet Wyman, Murdock said:

"I'd like a couple of days off."

Wyman puffed a little harder and felt an odd thrust of relief. "Sure," he said. "Why not? Delaney can take over your desk. Any special reason?"

"It's this Brady thing."

"Oh, yeah," said Wyman. "I understand he was a friend of yours."

"A very special friend."

"How does it look now?"

Murdock had it in mind to answer the question as briefly as possible, but once he began to talk he found it easy to continue. It was as though there was a certain therapeutic value in being able to unburden himself and Wyman was a good listener, nodding from time to time, not interrupting, putting aside the cigar when he found it had gone out.

"Okay," he said when Murdock finished. "You want to work with your friend Bacon down at homicide. It's a good idea. You've done all right in the past that way. So what do you need time off for? You'll be working, won't you?"

"But not for the *Courier.*"

Wyman leaned forward, his broad face wrinkled. "Why won't you?"

"I don't mean I won't bring it in if anything breaks," Murdock said stubbornly, "but for me this is a personal thing. The chances are I can't do much anyway, but I know the people and if I can help out I'll be doing it for myself, not the paper."

"What the hell," Wyman said, and now he grinned. "It's the same thing, ain't it? You're not working by the hour, are you? You don't come under the union rules."

"The murder of a man like Brady isn't worth more than a half column."

"With the Aldersons in it, it could be front page, and you know it." Wyman's chuckle was a warm and friendly sound. "If your conscience is bothering you for taking money for something you want to do for yourself, forget it."

He pushed back his chair and reached for the cigar. "Go on," he said. "Beat it. Grab yourself three or four drinks and go home and get some sleep. I'll put the word out that you won't be in."

Murdock pulled his legs in and stood up, cheered somehow by Wyman's manner and blunt words and already beginning to feel better. As he went to the door a feeling of new confidence began to stir inside him.

8

KENT MURDOCK had already transferred his camera and case and raincoat from the company car to his own before he had gone upstairs, and now he unlocked the door and climbed in. He wanted the drinks that Wyman had mentioned but since he had no desire to stand at a bar he decided to wait until he was home. As it turned out he had to wait a bit longer than he had anticipated because on the way home a new idea came to him and he took a detour that brought him back to the house where Tom Brady had lived.

It was not nostalgia that took him there but a knowledge of one detail that was known, so far as he knew, only to Brady and himself. The police had searched the apartment and found nothing of interest, but since it was unlikely they could know of the existence of a secret compartment in Brady's desk, there was still a chance that he might uncover something worth while.

That is what he thought as he entered the darkened vestibule and pushed open the inner door. He had no key to Brady's flat but he knew what kind of a lock it was and he had in his wallet an instrument given him a long time ago by another private detective named Jack Fenner.

He took it out as he paused in the half-light of the second-floor landing, a thin steel blade, rounded at one end and perhaps a half inch wide. He tried the knob first and found the door locked; after that it was a matter of seconds to insert the light but flexible blade between the moulding and the casing so that it engaged the sloping surface of the bolt.

When he felt it slide he turned the knob, and this time the latch clicked and the door was open. In no hurry now, he withdrew the blade and replaced it in his wallet. He opened the door and stepped silently inside and then, unaccountably, he froze there as the door swung behind him, the hand that started to reach for the electric switch checked in mid-air.

Neither then nor later could Murdock ever be sure what it was that warned him. He had not been conscious of any sound nor did he hear one now until he reached behind him to close the door and cut off the crack of light that seeped in from the hall.

Until then he'd had no premonition of danger and when, finally, it came he first repelled it by telling himself that it was nothing but imagination; that what he felt was due to nerves stretched too tight by the things that had happened that night.

Then he was moving in spite of himself, stepping lightly to one side and hunkering down to make himself small, the odd fear persisting as though some radar system of the mind was collaborating with instinct to tell him that he was not alone. Obeying this intuitive alarm he remained motionless, mouth open and breath held, ears straining and his senses sharply tuned until, from somewhere on his left, there came a whisper of sound to tell him that instinct had been right.

Because he knew this room almost as well as his own he located the sound at once, identifying it as the soft brushing of some weight across the nap of the rug. On his right two windows overlooked the street, the undefinable outlines indicating that the shades must have been pulled. On the left were two doorways, one leading to the bedroom and bath, the other to a dinette and kitchen. Beyond was another door which provided the only other way out of the apartment.

He started moving that way now, his memory of the floor plan and the placement of the furniture guiding him. That he might turn on the light and try a frontal assault did not occur to him, possibly because the image of the intruder which had grown in his mind had become that of a killer who had come here as he had, illegally and in stealth, to look for something important to him.

The one who had walked into Tom Brady's office had carried a gun. That was the assumption, and if true, it meant the killer still had a gun. And while Murdock had no intention of standing still while the other escaped by the rear stairway, he was no fool.

He moved with caution to the door of the dinette, hearing a metallic click in the darkness ahead, feeling now the stirring of air around his ankles. This told him the back door was open, and since he knew it had no patent closing device, he felt it would remain that way.

Not touching anything, relying solely on his memory, he moved with silent tread into the kitchen and across the linoleum floor. An outstretched hand found the edge of the open door, and when he stopped here to hold his breath again and listen, he heard the faint creaking of a stair tread below him.

Still keeping his distance he started down, his fingers touching the railing on his right. He reached a tiny landing where the stairs cut back to reach the second floor and now, starting down the last flight, he heard the door open and felt the quick rush of night air up the stair well.

He moved more quickly then until he reached the

ground floor. Stopping here as instinct cautioned him, he found the knob and turned it. He opened the door a two-inch crack and suddenly the night seemed brighter with the reflected glow of some street light. Not knowing what lay beyond he started to widen the crack. It was then that the shot came, the hammering sound of it simultaneous with the vibration of the door against his palm.

Murdock stood where he was as the door clicked shut from the impact of the slug which had buried itself somewhere above him. He did not know what lay outside, but for the first time he counted the odds and found them bad. He seemed to understand that the shot had been a warning one to keep him from following, but when he realized what might have happened had he opened the door wide in his pursuit he felt the perspiration break out under his arms and there was a sudden weakness in his knees.

He swore silently as he waited in the darkness. He called himself several kinds of fool, but even as he did so he wondered how else he could have acted. When he had counted off what seemed like a half minute he made another attempt to open the door, not because he expected to see anyone but just to know what was outside.

This time he was successful and as he stepped out he found himself in a narrow alley that was blind at one end and open at the other. For another moment he stood there, the perspiration drying coldly on his spine, and then he retraced his steps, mounting in the stuffy darkness until he came to Brady's kitchen.

He did not turn on a light until he reached the living room and again the feeling of depression and helplessness settled over him as he saw the familiar pieces: the worn davenport, the sagging leather chair, the tilt-top table they always used for pinochle, the ancient kneehole desk.

It was this desk that had brought him here, and because
he did not want to sit and brood, he went to it now, opening the bottom drawer on the right. At first glance this
seemed like nothing more than a receptacle for old check-
books and account books, but when he had removed them
and the drawer seemed empty he reached far back, hooked
the tip of his finger into a hole that had been cut across one
corner, and lifted.

The bottom, which was not the bottom but in reality
only a shelf, tipped up to reveal an inch-deep recess which
some unknown owner had fashioned many years ago.
Brady had not discovered it himself until a year ago and he
had shown it to Murdock one night, adding that this was
where he kept his valuables.

What Murdock found here now was a passbook on a
local savings bank and three legal-size envelopes. There
was nothing more, and when he had placed them on the
desk he studied them a moment before he opened them.

He had no feeling that he was prying into personal matters that were no concern of his. If he had thought about it
at all he would have known it was a duty because there
had once been an evening when Brady had told him that
if anything ever happened to him, Murdock was to see that
whatever was in the drawer was turned over to Alice, his
daughter, or to his lawyer.

Opening the bankbook first he saw that Brady had
twenty-two hundred and some dollars in his account. He
put it aside and picked up the first envelope, which was
unsealed and contained three E-bonds with a face value of
five hundred dollars each. The second envelope contained
an insurance policy for ten thousand dollars made out to
his daughter; the third was Brady's will.

Murdock's hands were unsteady as he opened this and

found it a simple one-page document drawn by a lawyer whose name was familiar. In effect it said that all personal property was to go to his daughter, that because of an insurance policy which had been made payable to her, the balance of his estate was to be held in trust for the education of his two grandchildren.

Murdock swallowed hard as he put the will in its proper envelope, the addition that came to his mind unconscious but inescapable. There was, he knew, a checking account but he did not think it would amount to much. Which meant that now, with Brady gone, what was left in worldly goods after a lifetime of hard work would add up to ten thousand dollars for his daughter—before funeral expenses —and perhaps four thousand for her children.

Murdock put the bankbook and the three envelopes back with care before he remembered that there was one more item that should be included: a bonus.

If Brady had lived it would have been paid, and suddenly it seemed terribly important that Murdock find those reports and collect from Harriett Alderson this bonus that she had promised. He told himself there must be some way and yet, even as he sat there, certain now that there was nothing here that would help him discover who had killed his friend, an unreasoning anger welled up inside him and he slammed the drawer and kicked the chair back as he came to his feet.

He snapped off the light and left the room, moving blindly down the stairs and out into the coolness of the night. He drove directly home because the need for the postponed drinks was very great now. He took out his camera and case and raincoat and locked the car; when he had let himself into his second-floor flat, he put his things aside and went directly to the kitchen.

The Scotch-on-rocks he made was very dark indeed, and he had just taken his first big swallow when the buzzer sounded. Scowling at the door and somehow resenting the sound, he crossed the room, not knowing just what to expect and not particularly caring. He opened the door wide, stepping back as he did so, and the two men who stood there moved forward together.

He knew at once that the two were strangers and as he moved aside to give them room he understood that they must have been waiting outside for his return. On the heels of this thought he recalled Sally Fisher's experience with two unseen hoodlums. He did not know yet if there was any connection but he had one more impression that was clear cut and definite: these two looked like trouble. Instinct born of long experience with all sorts of people told him this much, and such was his mood that he found himself looking forward to a little trouble with an unaccustomed eagerness.

He finished the rest of his drink and put the glass aside. Then, while they looked him over, he weighed each man in turn, finding one of them about his own height but thirty pounds heavier, a husky, thick-bodied man with a crooked nose, scarred brows, and not much neck. The other one was slicker looking, on the thin side and not much more than a welterweight, with a smooth swart skin and shiny black hair.

"Okay," he said. "What do you want?"

"A quick look," the thin man said. "In your pockets first, pal."

"Where's your gun?" Murdock said.

"We got one." The thin one tapped his pocket negligently. "But I don't think we'll need it. Eddie'll take care of things."

"You talk tough."

"You'll find out how tough if you get fancy."

Murdock's dark eyes were busy now, but he grinned as he asked if they knew what they were looking for.

"We'll let you know. Just get your arms up and stand still. . . . Watch him, Eddie."

By this time Murdock was ready to admit that the two were probably tough and could be brutal. He also knew that they were intent on demonstrating their toughness and this took him back to the days when he had played a little football in college. He had been up against certain tough ones then and he had learned that very often that type of player was so busy proving he was tough that it was easy to take him out of a play if you clipped him properly.

He remembered this now, his hands still hanging loosely, as Eddie stepped closer. When the thin lad moved round behind him, Murdock let his weight come forward, his eyes measuring the hard rock of Eddie's chin and deciding it might prove to be a discouraging target. He felt the thin one pat his outer pockets, bumping him a little, still acting tough, and finally slipping one hand under his armpit to feel the inside pocket.

That made it easier, especially for one who had learned a trick or two in the army.

Without moving anything except his one arm in that first instant, Murdock clamped it to his side, pinioning the thin man's arm above the elbow. Then, as Eddie awakened, Murdock turned and bent, still holding to the arm, finding the hand now and yanking it as he took the weight on his back.

Still pulling the hand, he heaved hard, hearing the

startled cry as the man's heels went high and his body crashed downward.

Eddie had to get out of the way or get hit and he reacted well for one who was not too bright. But he was slow. He had to set himself before he could throw his looping hook, and as his companion hit the floor on the back of his neck, Murdock stepped happily inside the loop of that swing. Concentrating on the second shirt button above the belt line, he drove his right into the bulging flesh with all his weight behind it.

Eddie said: "Ooosh," and doubled over, eyes bulging.

Before he could drop to his knees, Murdock spun to meet the stunned but rising tough lad. A short smart blow with the edge of his hand that caught the back of the thin neck knocked the fellow flat again and then Murdock reached for the gun, ripping the pocket half off as he jerked the automatic free.

There was no further trouble with Eddie.

Eddie was still on his knees, but doubled over, with his head nearly touching the floor and his hands hugging his middle. He was still gagging as he fought to get his breath, and as Murdock turned toward his camera there was a spring in his stride and his grin was elated, not for what he had accomplished, since this had not been difficult, given a certain technique and a proper understanding of his foe, but because the physical effort was a tonic that had helped to lift his spirits.

There was already a bulb in the flash gun and when he had checked the aperture and shutter speed he stepped back and focused on Eddie, who was sitting up now, glowering but still a little green. The thin one was also sitting up, cursing viciously as he rubbed the back of his neck.

"Stay there!" Murdock said. "Stay put, both of you!"

He took his picture, put the camera aside and inspected the gun. He did not think it had been fired recently but it held a full clip and there was a bullet in the chamber. He pointed it at the pair as he lifted the telephone and dialed a number.

"Bacon," he said when he had his connection, "when're you going home?"

"I've got my hat and coat on now."

"Then listen to this," said Murdock and began to speak his piece, at the same time reminding the lieutenant of what had happened to Walt Carey. "There could be a connection," he said, "but I doubt it. Whoever came to the studio got those films. I think this pair wanted the ones I took for Brady."

"It makes more sense that way," Bacon said. "You don't know who they are?"

"No."

"Okay, I'll send over for them. I'll see they get a session tonight and in the morning I'll have a go at 'em myself. . . ."

The two men Bacon sent over made a contrasting pair, one of them being a blunt-nosed man of fifty or so and the other much younger, with curly dark hair and an expansive manner. He was the one who gave the two captives a routine search while Murdock handed the automatic to his companion and explained what had happened. This one seemed to know Murdock, though Murdock could not recall his name.

"You took the two of 'em, hunh?" he said.

"They were careless," Murdock said. "They wanted to show me how tough they were."

"If they're that tough," the detective said in a voice that

seemed sardonically amused, "maybe you'd better put the cuffs on, Harry."

Eddie submitted without a word as his right wrist was shackled to the left one of the thin lad. He had not opened his mouth since he entered, but his associate made up for the lack of conversation.

"You got nothing on us," he said.

"How about breaking and entering?" the detective said.

"You can't make it stick. We buzzed the buzzer and this guy let us in. We just wanted to talk to him."

"Assault, maybe?"

"That's a laugh. We never laid a hand on him. He's the one that started the rumble. We'll sign a complaint."

"I'll bet." The detective grinned and indicated the gun in his hand. "What about this? Got a permit?"

That stopped the thin one for a moment. "I had one," he said, not too convincingly. "Maybe it's home."

"Then you'll have a chance to produce it. . . . Come on," he said, taking the other's arm and giving it a twist. "Let's meander. It's getting late and I guess Mr. Murdock would like to go to bed."

He helped his companion nudge the two into the hall and before he closed the door, he said: "The Lieutenant says you'll be around in the morning, right?"

Murdock said yes and just then the thin man took up his protest. "You gotta book us or release us," he said, as though he had learned the words by rote.

"How about disorderly conduct?" The older detective gave a yank at his arm. "If you give me any more yap I'll personally make it resisting an officer in the performance of his duties." And with that, he winked and went out.

Murdock still felt good as he replenished his drink and then came back to the door to snap on the night latch. He put a new bulb in the flash gun and reversed the film holder. He set the focus at twelve feet—the way he usually kept it—and the shutter at ¼oo. He picked up his raincoat and when he went to hang it up he saw the dark smudge in the back between the shoulders. He stared at it a moment, muttering because he'd had it cleaned two weeks earlier. Then, remembering how he had tossed it on the shelf behind the back seat of his car and used it as a pillow on the printing room floor, he decided it was his own fault.

Ten minutes later he was in bed, but it took him a while to get to sleep. He was unable to smother the workings of his mind, but no longer did his thoughts center exclusively on Tom Brady; instead he considered the copies he had made that afternoon. As he concentrated, forgotten details came back to him. There had been something about a woman named Ruth Colby and a man named Benjamin Danton, but the name that bothered him most was that of Jerry Alderson.

Jerry Alderson, the extroverted and fun-loving bachelor of the Alderson clan, the one who explained his single state by saying that he couldn't marry without his mother's approval. It made a good joke, but although Murdock could not prove it, it seemed to him that a marriage license had been signed by a Jerry Alderson in San Francisco in 1951. The Jerry Alderson he knew? Or someone who had used his name?

9

KENT MURDOCK was toweling briskly after his shower at nine o'clock the following morning when he heard the buzzer. He stopped his toweling and stood naked and tousle-headed for a second or two, some annoyance mixed with the indecision in his dark gaze. When the sound was repeated with more persistence, he grabbed a pair of shorts, slipped into them, and reached for his robe. He had it belted by the time he opened the door to find Sally Fisher standing there.

If she was at all embarrassed by his attire she did not show it. She wore a neat flannel suit, her chestnut hair was soft and shining, and her hazel eyes had a look of excitement in them.

"I'm sorry if I was too early," she said quickly, "but I had to ask you something before I went to the office."

Murdock closed the door and followed her into the room, conscious of his bare shanks but reassured when he saw that she was more interested in the apartment than she was in him.

"This is nice," she said. "I like it. I've never been here before, have I? . . . I know I haven't."

Still a little puzzled by her appearance, Murdock watched her make a circuit of the room, her glance approving until she caught sight of herself in a wall mirror. Then, stopping abruptly, she leaned forward and made a face at herself.

"My goodness," she said, and came back to get the handbag she had deposited on the table near the door.

"What?" said Murdock.

"My mouth. It's crooked."

By that time she had extracted her lipstick and returned to the mirror. Then, her lips twisting this way and that, working with lipstick and finger tip, she made repairs. When she finished she put the lipstick down, glanced at her finger, and came back to search for a tissue.

"I thought of some things," she said.

Murdock's reaction was still sluggish. "Did you?"

"Like the lieutenant asked me to last night."

"Oh . . . Good."

"And I stopped to ask if you think I should tell him about them. Or should I tell you—or what?"

"Tell Bacon," Murdock said, "definitely."

"Will it be pretty awful down there at police headquarters? I mean, will there be a lot of men sitting around and—"

Murdock laughed. He said it would not be awful. "You'll sit in an office, or a room like any other room, and talk to Bacon or maybe a stenographer."

She was standing in front of him now, still not noticing his bare legs but smiling up at him, her young face sweetly attractive and her red mouth straight.

"All right," she said, "I'll do it on my way to work. Where do I go? In the building, I mean."

"The easiest way is to stop at the information desk in the lobby and tell the man who you are and who you want to see."

"I will." She tucked her bag under her arm and went to the door and now, for the first time, her carefree manner slipped away and her eyes grew serious. "I didn't remember such an awful lot. I don't know if it will help—"

Murdock said all she had to do was tell what she could

and let the police decide if it would help. He eased her into
the hall, resisting the impulse to give her a small pat on the
trim curve of her hip. He closed the door and blew out his
breath, grinning a little as he went into the kitchen and
turned the heat off under the coffee. When he had put a
stale piece of bread in the toaster, he gulped his juice and
hurried into the bedroom where he put on socks, trousers,
shirt, and shoes before he heard the toaster pop.

He had one cup of coffee with his toast and marmalade
and brought a second cup back to the bedroom while he
knotted a dark-blue tie, buttoned the collar points, and
combed his hair. From his closet he selected a Shetland
jacket and then went back to the kitchen to rinse his dishes.

Twenty minutes later he walked into a bare and uninviting room furnished with some worn tables and chairs,
two of which were occupied by a couple of detectives who
were in conference about something. The third man was
banging away at a typewriter and he looked up long
enough to nod when Murdock gestured at the closed door
of Bacon's inner sanctum.

As an office it was no more appealing than Murdock's
cubby, though there was room for two extra chairs. Bacon,
who had been busy contemplating the grimy window,
swiveled the desk chair and scowled at his caller, not with
any animosity but simply as a matter of routine. He
watched Murdock sit down and then reached into a drawer
to take out a cigar, a thin and unprepossessing creation
which he bought by the box for five cents apiece under the
trade name of Little Wonder Panatelas.

"Did Sally Fisher come in?" Murdock asked.

"She's spilling it to a policewoman."

"What about those two characters your men dragged in
last night?"

Bacon used a penknife to manicure the end of his cigar, giving it the same care he might have used on an imported fifty-center. Waiting until he had lighted it with the same loving care, he expelled smoke from his mouth and said:

"Small-time hoods. A bouncer and a part-time bartender. Minor records—mostly assault. Nothing heavy."

"It's too bad Sally didn't see the two that jumped her."

"Yeah."

"If it's the same two, they didn't think it up themselves."

"No."

"That leaves two possibilities. One, they were told to get the films because whoever hired them didn't get them from Brady; two, it was known the girl copied Brady's reports."

"I can't buy the film thing," Bacon said.

"Why?"

"Because Brady didn't ask her to pick them up from your desk in the first place. If he didn't ask her it wasn't in his mind, so how could anyone figure she *did* pick them up. Those punks could have come to you for films because a lot of people knew you were taking pictures. Not her."

Bacon's reasoning was sound and Murdock admitted it. "All right, then say they went to Sally's to get the reports."

"Whoever killed Brady took the reports," Bacon said.

"But could the killer know he had them all? Could he be sure there were no rough copies around? Who besides me knew she did that copying?"

"Kirby."

"He doesn't fit."

"Why?"

"Because he knew Brady always took the roughs from Sally along with the finished copies. He knew the roughs were destroyed, and if he wanted the reports he could have jimmied the file or had a key made. He could have taken them while he was waiting for the police."

"I guess you're right. So who else knew about her?"

"Arthur Enders could have known. He knew how Brady worked. As a lawyer he might know where to hire a couple of hoods."

"The trouble is we don't know who else Brady talked to. Hell, he could have told a lot of people about a girl named Fisher who lived in his building and did his copying."

Murdock thought it over, wondering if he should tell what happened at Brady's apartment the night before. Deciding it could do no good now, he let his thoughts move on until Bacon said:

"Frank Kirby's coming in a little later, so if you want to kick this around a little more, now's the time."

"Kirby?" Murdock said with some surprise. "Are you figuring him for this?"

"Kirby was there," Bacon said, talking now between small, delicate puffs. "Kirby knew Tom was working for the Aldersons. He knew Tom had come to you to make copies of those documents or whatever they were."

He rolled the cigar between his lips and said: "Kirby was a pretty fair cop. He could have been a hell of a good one; he made some damn good pinches and he was only in trouble once. But he fought the regulations and the discipline. Every now and then he'd get hotheaded and pop off but he was smart and capable—" He broke off and said: "Tom ever talk to you about him?"

"Not often," Murdock said. "He had the same picture you've got, but he admitted that he and Kirby didn't look at this private work the same way. Tom was older and all he wanted to do was keep busy and pick up some extra money. Kirby thought he could get some place and he was willing to try. He'd take divorce cases Tom wouldn't touch. Tom said it wasn't just the money with Kirby—though that was important—so much as the desire to get some place, to be important."

"Yeah," said Bacon. "Well, for your information, there's nothing on this one that ties Kirby in. We had a look at his place last night while he was out. He's got two guns all right, but there were no reports or a briefcase or anything else that seemed out of line. I found out he's got a little money in the bank and he's got no charge accounts. Unless there was one hell of a lot of dough involved you can't make Kirby fit; after all, he was a cop too."

"What about alibis?"

"Hah!" said Bacon and puffed a little harder on his pan-atela. "The only one who's clear is the old lady and I think that butler would probably lie for her."

"She needs a cane to walk."

"So what?" He made noises in his throat and said: "Take this Donald. He goes to the factory. The night watchman says he was there at eight thirty, but who pays the night watchman?"

Murdock stretched out in his chair, dark eyes thoughtful but amused as he watched Bacon.

"You don't believe anybody, do you?"

"Not when it's murder, son. Not when it's murder. . . . Rita, the blonde one, has got no alibi at all. She went for a walk. . . . Gloria, the other daughter-in-law, said she ate at the Ritz, and she did. But not alone."

"Oh?" Murdock waited, aware that Bacon was eyeing him narrowly. "Arthur Enders?"

"Right. They left together sometime after eight thirty but we haven't been able to pin point the time. I don't know when she got back to the Alderson place, but if it was the

wrong time the old lady would probably lie for her too.
. . . We gave Enders's apartment a fast frisk," he said.

"When?" said Murdock, his surprise showing but approval in his mind.

"When we were all at Aldersons', when do you think?
That's why it was fast. . . . No reports," he added sourly.
"No briefcase. We can't tackle the office until we produce
a warrant and how could you find anything in a law office
anyway? They probably got files on four thousand different things."

"What about Jerry?"

"All we know for sure about Jerry is that his story about
the Club Saville checks. He was there at nine fifteen. We
gave his place the same treatment we gave Enders's and
got the same result. Nothing." He tipped ashes into the
wastebasket and his voice grew blunt. "What I'd like to do
is give that Alderson place a real going over."

Murdock had been paying attention and his mind had
not been idle. Now, feeling his way, he said:

"Suppose someone got those reports, maybe in the briefcase, and was afraid to take them home. It would be sort of
stupid, wouldn't it, if there was any chance your place
would be searched?"

"Go ahead," Bacon said. "I'm tuned in."

"You grab the reports and you need a safe place to hide
them in, maybe only for a day or so." He half closed one
eye as he hesitated. "From Brady's office to the Back Bay
station is only a block and a half. A man could duck over
there fast and use one of those parcel lockers—"

He let the thought remain unfinished because of the
changing expression on Bacon's face. The mouth twitched
once and the gray eyes narrowed slightly, their expression
amused and, it seemed, approving.

"Well?" he said, with mild defiance.

"Yeah," said Bacon, his grin expanding. "You know when you put your mind to it you think real good. . . . We went there," he said. "Last night. My man routed out the guy with the keys and opened every damn locker." He grunted and put his cigar back in his mouth.

"Came up with four briefcases," he said. "One had somebody's lunch in it, one was full of samples, one had some dirty laundry in it; the last one must have belonged to an insurance salesman because it was full of forms and rate books, things like that."

Murdock shrugged, reminded once again of the lieutenant's thoroughness. He started to rise and Bacon waved him back.

"We got just one good lead," he said. "Came across it when we checked the tenants in the building. One of 'em is a guy with a one-man accounting office at the third floor front. He was working late and as he came downstairs he saw a woman looking at the office directory tacked to the wall."

"When was that?"

"About nine o'clock, and that checks because he says it started to pour right after he went out. . . . Well, anyway, he gave this dame a second look and knew she didn't belong in the building so he stopped to ask if he could help her. He asked if she was looking for someone—she wore dark glasses and he wasn't sure she could read the directory—and she said she was looking for Mr. Brady's office. He told her where it was."

Bacon leaned back, puffing contentedly while he contemplated the cracked calcimine above his desk. His attitude suggested he would say no more until pressed but before he did so Murdock voiced an objection.

"A woman coming there with murder in her mind wouldn't be telling a tenant who she was looking for."

"Who says anybody went there with murder in his mind? Does it have to be that way?" Bacon demanded. "For all we know the killer went there hoping to make a deal and found he couldn't sell the idea to Brady."

"Okay, who was the woman?"

"I wish I knew." Bacon sighed aloud. "Sort of tall, according to the accountant, and wore a camel's-hair coat. Young. He's pretty sure of that. The trouble is, it's a relative term. How young is young? Don't know if she was blonde or brunette because she wore a scarf. Add the dark glasses, the fact that the light in the hall was bad, and that she never once looked at him, and what've we got?"

Murdock stood up and Bacon said: "If we could get those Aldersons to come clean we might get somewhere. You know the tribe. Why don't you dig around and give me a hand on this? Brady was a friend of yours, too."

He took the cigar from his mouth and then, as though the name had uncovered some forgotten facet of his mind, his gaze grew remote and his voice was reflective.

"A hell of a guy, Brady," he said. "Solid. Not only as a person but as a cop. If we had a whole department like him this would be a better town. It wasn't just that he was honest in everything he did—it was the way he felt about his job. He liked being a detective. That's all he wanted. I don't think he used a gun more than two or three times in his life, but when he had to be was a very handy guy with his fists. Hated crooks but was always ready to help a decent guy who just happened to make a mistake. Even the guys he collared liked him."

That was a lot of talk for Bacon. Considering the source this was a very great tribute and it suddenly occurred to

Murdock that such praise applied to Bacon as well. Bacon perhaps lacked some of Brady's warmth, but he had the same basic integrity, the same attitude toward his work. Murdock would never dare say so, but that was what he was thinking when someone knocked at the door and brought his thoughts back to the moment.

The detective who stuck his head in said Frank Kirby was outside. Bacon said: "Okay," and Murdock moved out. As he met Kirby coming in the detective put a hand on his arm.

"I phoned your office and they said you weren't in," he said. "Where'll you be in—say an hour?"

"Probably at the office," Murdock said.

"I'll be over," Kirby said. "I want to talk to you."

10

WHEN Murdock walked into the studio a few minutes later he was surprised to see Delaney at his desk because he had forgotten what he had told T. A. Wyman the night before. Now Delaney looked a bit embarrassed and said he had been told Murdock would not be in.

"Do you want to get here?" he asked, half rising.

"No," Murdock said. "Sit still."

He backed out of the doorway, feeling a little lost as he glanced round the studio. In retrospect he was a little embarrassed himself, not about Delaney but about the things he had said to Wyman. For it occurred to him now that he had probably sounded like a schoolboy with his request for a couple of days off and the inference that he needed the time to solve Brady's murder.

Because he was annoyed with himself he moved over behind a cabinet partition that had been erected behind his office. Here the shelves had been cut up into boxlike receptacles much like mailboxes behind a hotel desk only larger. Each was marked with a photographer's name and served as a catchall for small personal items and mail. Extending out from this was a broader shelf that made a long continuous table the men used as a desk when making notes or writing captions. There was a chair here by the window and Murdock eased down in it.

"Two days," he said, talking silently to himself. "For what? Bacon's already checked Brady's building, and the parcel lockers in the station. He's probably working on the taxi companies to see if that woman in the camel's-hair coat got a ride. So go ahead and solve the case, Murdock. Get busy."

His thoughts continued in a like vein until he got the subject out of his system, and then, becoming more sensible, he reached for the telephone and asked the operator to get him the hospital. It took him a while to locate the resident who had been looking after Carey, but when he asked his questions the answers were good.

"He'll be okay," the doctor said. "If he behaves himself we'll release him tomorrow, but no visitors until late this afternoon or this evening."

"Can I talk to him?"

"It would be better if you didn't."

Murdock hung up, feeling slightly better. He got a cigarette going and then he sat there sorting out facts and details he could substantiate, but never going far with his speculations. He paid no attention to the traffic in and out of the studio as members of the staff came and went. When spoken to, his hellos were automatic so that it surprised him a little when someone took hold of his shoulder and he looked round to find Kirby standing there.

"Where can we talk?" Kirby said. "Is it too early for lunch?"

Murdock said he guessed this was as good a time as any, so they rode down in the elevator and went round the corner to this place that made up in plain, well-cooked food for what it lacked in style. It had not yet begun to fill up with luncheon customers and they found a corner table, and presently a waiter—they all were ancient males who were no more polite than they had to be—came to ask their pleasure. After Murdock had ordered soup and a sandwich and Kirby had asked for broiled scrod and French fries, Kirby spoke of the things he had in mind.

He wanted to know if Murdock had any idea who killed Brady, and if he thought he could solve the case. Murdock said no to both questions.

"And neither can anybody else, alone," Kirby said, "unless someone gets awfully damn lucky. Take me, I'm a private cop now and I've got no authority and I'll get no help from the department. Murder is a police job and always will be, but in this one I'd like a piece of it if I can get it and I think you would too, right?"

Murdock nodded in agreement as he sampled his soup.

"The police have got the manpower, the technical equipment, the authority," Kirby said, "but they're not God. Some people fight 'em, and clam up; some don't. All right, I was a cop too and I've got my own ways of working. I can do some things the police can't do because I've got no hardheaded captain to worry about any more. The same with you. With that press card of yours you can get in places where I couldn't get past the front steps. Not only that, people will talk to a newspaper guy where they won't talk to a cop."

He watched the waiter put down the scrod, squeezed lemon on it, and coated the potatoes with catsup. Murdock waited, noticing Kirby's houndstooth jacket, the slight upward-slanting angle of his brows, the way the muscles of the hard jaw bulged as he chewed. He recalled the things that had been said about the man, and the impression remained that here was a very competent, ambitious fellow who would be a good man to have on your side and very difficult to push very far. As he considered such details the gray-green eyes came up to meet his, steady, direct, and confident.

"You know about my record on the force," he said, and now his mouth twisted as he added: "I had a bellyful of it. Twelve years. I liked the work, but not the silly rigmarole you have to put up with. I got a hole in my thigh when I shot it out with those three punks that tried to hold up the delicatessen; I was flat on the sidewalk when I dropped the third one. For that I got a promotion out of uniform. I'm a credit to the department with a citation and a bronze medal."

Murdock's cold roast-beef sandwich came and he began to work on it, at the same time nodding to indicate that he was still listening.

"I had some good pinches," Kirby said. "I'm third from top on the sergeant's list. So what happens? A guy crashes a car I peg as stolen. He gets out and runs when I yell at him. It's at night so how do I know who he is or how long a record he's got? I throw a slug over his head to warn him and when he keeps going I bring him down. That's what I'm paid to do but this time it turns out to be a kid without any previous record, so there's a big stink and I get a department trial, an official reprimand."

"You weren't suspended," Murdock said.

"Or demoted. Not at the time. I was too hot. So when I cool off I get a transfer to—guess where?"

"Hyde Park."

"Yeah," said Kirby and grinned. "You read the papers. . . . Okay, so I quit. I was sore."

"Maybe too sore," Murdock said, "because I don't think anyone in the department really blamed you for what you did. It was just your bad luck that the kid happened to have no record. It was the publicity that made you hot."

"And who makes this publicity?"

"We do," Murdock admitted. "The newspapers. Because the boy's family and friends began calling in and writing letters. To them it was an illustration of police brutality, and yet they're the same ones who demand something be done to curb juvenile delinquency when someone else's kids are involved. The department had to make some kind of a show to cool things off and you took it personally—"

"Wouldn't you?"

"Ten years ago when I was that much younger and that much more stubborn and hotheaded, yes. Now I think I'd try to ride with it."

"That's the philosophical approach, hunh?" Kirby tipped one hand. "Well, you're probably right. But it's over the dam, so the hell with it. Also this is a lot of talk, but I'm leading up to something and I want to put it all on the line. . . . You want to nail the one who killed Brady because he was a friend, right?

"I'm not going to kid you," he said, not waiting for a reply. "I'm not going to tell you he was an old friend of mine, because it's not true. We weren't that close and prob-

ably never would be because we didn't think alike. He was
getting old and he wanted to keep busy and I want to get
someplace. But just the same he gave me a hand when I
needed it. He let me share his office for free until I could
pay my half. He put in a good word for me here and there
and I'm not likely to forget it. But I'd be a liar if I said that
was the only reason I'd like to have a hand in cracking this
one."

He pushed his dish aside and said: "I've got a couple of
accounts of my own. Now I'll probably keep handling the
ones I took over for Tom while he was away. Pretty soon
I'll be able to take someone in with me. If I keep plugging
I hope to get a real nice little agency. I like the work. I
wouldn't have started out a cop if I didn't feel that way.
You want to crack the case for Tom; I want to crack it
partly for Tom but mostly for me. If that sounds a little
cold-blooded that's the way it is and you're too smart a guy
for me to try to kid."

Such frankness impressed Murdock. He felt that Kirby
meant what he said and, considering the character of the
man as he knew it, the statement did not sound cold-
blooded. Kirby was ambitious and he was thinking of
Kirby.

"What you really mean is that you could use a little publicity," he said.

Kirby's grin came again, but the eyes remained intent
as he nodded.

"If I can help," he said. "You're the press. I'm talking to
one of the top guys. You'll know—if the case is cracked at
all—whether I've put anything in the pot. If I have I know
you'll see I get a couple of lines. I know that without having to ask for it. But my point is this: will you co-operate?
Or maybe that's not the way to put it. What I mean is, if

you have something you don't want to go to the police with, but you still need help, will you let me see what I can do?"

Murdock said yes, and meant it. He said the trouble was that he had no idea what he could do next. He said there were only two things he could tell Kirby that Kirby did not already know, and mentioned first the incident at Brady's apartment.

Kirby's gray-green eyes opened wide and his lips whistled softly. "I'll be damned," he said. "You could have got yourself killed."

"I probably would have if I had turned on the light."

"That's for sure. You had him trapped. Once you got a look at him he'd have to shoot." He shook his head, his brows furrowed. "But why?" he said. "You knew the cops had searched the place."

Murdock said he knew now that it was a bad idea, but at the time he thought there might be a chance the police had overlooked something.

"Also," he said, "I had a couple of callers when I got home, probably the same ones who searched Sally Fisher's place and snatched her bag."

He went on to explain what had happened and what Bacon had said about the two thugs. He said he did not know their names but that Bacon did.

"They'll be out on bail some time today," he added. "Bacon thinks there's a chance they might lead him to the one who hired them."

"On that," Kirby said, "maybe I can help. I can find out who they are and I've got some contacts that might be able to tip me off. . . . Yeah," he said thoughtfully, "that's all right. That could be a lead."

He was quicker than Murdock when the waiter presented the check. "Don't argue," he said, when Murdock protested. "This is mine. I'm the guy that's asking the favor." He put a half dollar on the table and pushed back his chair. "If you've got nothing better to do," he said, "you could think about the Aldersons. You can work on them from the inside because you know them. If you need any help outside just say so."

He grinned and said: "I wouldn't mind investigating that blonde. What's her name—Rita? She's a real doll. . . . I'll stop by later in the day," he said, "and we can compare notes. Okay?"

Murdock found he had a second caller when he returned to the studio. Delaney saw him come in and stopped him long enough to say that a woman was waiting for him.

"She didn't give her name," he said. "Said she was an old friend of yours."

Murdock stepped round the jutting partition and found her sitting in the chair by the window, a nice-looking woman of thirty or so, beginning to look a little matronly now but still having the nice complexion and the erect, well-moulded figure Murdock remembered. She was dressed in black—dress, coat, and hat. Her name was Alice —he could not recall her married name—and she was Tom Brady's daughter.

She rose when she saw him and let him take both of her hands. For an instant her dark eyes were misty, but she blinked back the tears and worked on a smile. When she finally spoke her voice was quiet but controlled and she seemed to have her emotions in hand.

"Hello, Kent."

Murdock did not know what to say. Many things went through his mind in that moment, but all seemed so inadequate and unsatisfactory that all he could do was repeat the greeting.

"Hello, Alice."

He glanced round, needing time and knowing they could not talk here. "Come on," he said, "let's get out of here." And then he had her by the arm, guiding her back to the elevators and riding to the fifth floor, where a row of partitioned offices had been erected opposite the elevators for the use of certain specialists. One of the smaller ones had been assigned to an editorial writer who was seldom in at that time of day, and when Murdock found it empty they stepped inside.

"They telephoned last night," she said, and sat down, her gaze averted, as though she was not quite ready to face him and wanted to spare him the effort of expressing his sympathy. "Someone from the police," she said.

Murdock watched her a moment and then he, too, had to look away. His face was hot and his hands were sweaty and he had to swallow to clear the hardness from his throat. He still did not know how to express the things he felt, but he had to try.

"I don't know what to say," he said huskily.

"I know you don't, Kent. It's too early yet and it isn't necessary because I know how you felt about Dad."

"Have you talked to anyone?"

"Only Dad's lawyer. I wanted to see you first. I—I thought you could tell me how it happened."

Murdock took a small breath, wondering where to begin. Then he hunched forward with his forearms on his knees and his gaze fixed and sightless. Not bothering with the incidents that had happened later, he told what had happened at Brady's office. When he finished she asked if the police knew who did it and he had to say no. It was then that she took the letter from her handbag.

"Dad stopped overnight with us on his way up from Florida," she said. "He wrote this letter before he left there and I brought it along because I hoped it might help." She looked down at the folded sheets and bit her lip.

"I'm afraid it isn't very definite," she said, "because he always insisted that what he did for others was confidential. He never wrote any of the particulars but he did mention things that gave us an idea of what sort of case he was working on. Mostly, I think, because he wanted us to know he kept busy."

"Did he say anything about this last job when you saw him?"

"Only that it was the biggest one he ever had. He seemed very proud of what he had done and he said there'd be a nice bonus and for us to think of something we needed for the house."

Her mouth trembled as she finished and now she was unfolding the letter and examining the two sheets. One of these, apparently dealing with personal things, she refolded and returned to the envelope; the other she passed to Murdock.

"This is about as close as he ever came to being specific. . . . No, don't read it now," she said, and started to rise. "When you get time. It probably isn't anything, anyway. . . . I'll be at the Sheraton, Kent."

"What can I do?" Murdock said as he came to his feet. "I can take care of everything if you—"

She smiled as she interrupted. "The lawyer will see to things," she said. "I understand the—the body will be released tomorrow and I thought the day after would be all right for the funeral. The lawyer said he thought that some

of Dad's friends from the police department might want
to—" She swallowed and tried again. "Perhaps you'd like to
be one of the pallbearers."

Murdock had to clear his throat before he could say yes,
and again there was that stinging in his eyes. Then she
was at the door, telling him that she could find her way out.
She did not look at him again and he did not insist, watching her standing there holding her shoulders back and her
chin up until the elevator came and the door closed.

He swore softly as he came back to the office and when
he found it did nothing to relieve his black mood of depression, he sat down and opened the sheet which proved to be
a piece of hotel stationery.

The letter was typewritten. The many mistakes were
blocked out rather than erased, but the phrasing was un-
mistakably Brady's. When Murdock had read it through
he began again more slowly.

*. . . no question about this being the biggest case I ever
worked on but I'm not sure I'd want to handle another like
it.*

*I guess my trouble is that I'm getting old and I think too
much. It's all right when I'm actually working because the
job is a challenge and I'm using the tricks of the trade I
learned as a cop. It's when I turn in the reports that I wonder.*

*Take this one I'm finishing up. I guess you'd say it was a
family matter where the mother—a wealthy one—isn't satisfied to let her kids alone but has to try to dominate everyone. What happens when, instead of leaving well enough
alone, she finds out one of her sons had a marriage she
didn't know anything about, that one of her daughters-in-
law maybe isn't a daughter-in-law at all and that the other*

*one stayed a month at the same hotel the family lawyer
happened to be staying at?*

*When I think of the trouble I'm making for a lot of peo-
ple I sometimes wish I hadn't started. Sometimes I think
I'd like to tear up what I have and give her back my salary
and expenses. The only trouble is I don't have that much
to spare and I accepted the job and I suppose I'm obli-
gated to handle it in good faith. And anyway just because
she wants to play God is no reason I should. But you see
there's more to my work than you'd think.*

*One thing, I'll be able to spend the night with you and
Fred on my way North, and will I be glad to see the two
children.*

With love,

Murdock put the letter in his pocket, no longer thinking
about the man who had written the words, but about their
significance. When he saw how the reference in the letter
supplemented the fragmentary knowledge he had gained
from the documents he had photographed, he knew what
he wanted to do. Stepping to the desk, he picked up the
telephone and asked for an outside line.

11

HENDERSON, the Alderson butler and houseman, was
wearing his daytime regalia—a linen jacket—when he
opened the door in response to Murdock's ring. Satisfied
that his visitor was acceptable, he made his customary
small bow and stepped back to open the door wider.

"Good afternoon, Mr. Murdock," he said in his soft-voiced way. "Mrs. Alderson is in the library. I think you know your way."

Murdock thanked him and climbed to the second floor, turning right in the hall away from the drawing room. As he approached the doorway opposite the stairs to the floor above, Rita Alderson appeared, her smile vague and her dark-blue eyes speculative.

"Hello," she said. "If you're going to be as serious as you sounded over the phone, maybe we'd better go up to my rooms."

Murdock followed her up the next flight, appreciating the curve of her calves but not dwelling on them. Again she turned right and he knew that this floor consisted of two suites, the one at the rear and overlooking the river belonging to Harriett Alderson while the front one was shared by Donald and Gloria. Rita occupied the top floor, rear, her suite consisting of a tiny sitting room and a bedroom beyond with connecting bath.

"Sit down," she said when she had closed the door. "Could you use a drink?"

The offer surprised Murdock, but when he considered his mission he decided a drink might help. He said that would be very nice and Rita stepped to a highboy and took out a bottle of Scotch.

"My private stock," she said. "For solitary drinking. There's no ice up here," she added. "Harriett wouldn't approve of daytime tippling."

She disappeared into the bedroom and Murdock could hear water running and the clink of glass. When she came back she held two old-fashioned glasses nearly full. She watched him over the rim of her drink as she tasted it and then she sat down on a chaise with a brocaded cover and spread her skirts.

She was wearing a navy wool dress, cut simply except for the rounded neckline which was, for her, attractively low, and now, because he liked this girl and found her long-lashed eyes disturbing, he was not sure just how to begin.

"I found out a few things since we talked yesterday afternoon," he said finally.

"And you want to talk about them, is that it? Did Mr. Brady actually come and ask you to take some pictures for him?"

"Yes."

"And what did you find out?"

"Not nearly enough," Murdock said, and spoke of the things Brady had said. "I remembered a few things," he added, "and a while ago I saw a letter he'd written to his daughter. That told me a little more."

"I see." She sipped her drink and put the glass on the small table beside her, picking up a silver cigarette box as she did so and waving him back as he started to rise to give her a light. She used the table lighter and leaned back. "And did you come here because you think I can help, or because you think I'm involved, or because of some story you want for your paper?"

Murdock considered the questions and found himself on the defensive. With no single concrete objective in mind, he saw that it was going to be difficult to put his intentions into words. Before he could reply, she resumed the offensive.

"You want to find out who killed Mr. Brady, don't you?"

"I intend to do what I can."

"Because you liked him and he was an old friend of

yours. . . . And what about me?" she said when he hesitated. "Am I a friend too?"

"You know you are."

"Because of George."

Murdock was honest about it as he recalled how George
Alderson had first introduced him to Rita when they came
down one week-end from Ogunquit.

"In the beginning, yes," he said, his smile thoughtful.
"After that you were on your own."

"That's a nice way of putting it," she said, "and I'm not
going to be coy with you. I liked you the first time I met
you and when I got to know you—remember how we used
to go out on the sloop, and the week-end the three of us
sailed across Cape Cod Bay and through the canal and
down Buzzard's Bay to Woods Hole?—I found I liked you
even more, though I couldn't tell you why."

She tapped ashes in a tray and said: "Maybe because
you kept your hands to yourself and always treated me like
the wife of a friend. I never had the feeling that you liked
me just because I had a reasonably pretty face and a better
than average figure. I mean, when you talked to me you
talked to me not just as a woman but as a woman who interested you as a person, if you know what I mean. I don't
know what it is that makes women like you—I'm pretty
sure most of them do—but I think it's more than being
just physically attractive, and you are; I think maybe it's
because you know how to talk to them. I'll bet it's just as
easy for you to be nice to some tired chorus girl and make
her feel important as it is to talk to some woman who really
is important and wants to be impressed."

The thought might have been more expertly phrased but
it was one of the nicest things that had been said to Murdock in a long time, pleasing him secretly but at the same

time warning him that he must not let the tribute influence
his thinking. He said he was glad she felt that way but
maybe she would have other ideas before he finished.
Then, taking the bit in his teeth, he said:

"I came here because there are some things I'd like to
know. Maybe you can help and maybe not, and maybe you
don't want to help. That's all right too, Rita, because Brady
was working for Harriett and what he found out may have
been responsible for his death. The police think that someone in the family is involved and so do I."

"Suppose I killed him," she said, with surprising candor.

Murdock blinked at her, not knowing whether to smile
or not but playing it straight.

"I don't think that," he said. "I'm going to be awfully
sorry if you did."

"But it wouldn't make any difference? I mean you'd still
tell the police."

"You'd have a better chance with a jury than most
women," he said dryly. "But it's a little silly, isn't it? Bringing that up now. Why don't you just work on that drink
and let me ask the questions. Then you can decide whether
you want to answer them or not. You grew up in California,
didn't you? Were you born there?"

"No."

"You were married out there—"

"And divorced," she said. "After one pretty awful year.
You've read about these women who are always getting
knocked around by their husbands? I mean really beaten?"

"I've seen several of them."

"Well, you're looking at another." She put her cigarette
out and took another swallow of her drink. "I never knew
my father," she said. "He ran away when I was a child. I
guess I was about ten when my mother married again and

my stepfather lasted six years before he took off. I guess you couldn't blame him. My mother was—"

She broke off and made a face. "But that's not important, is it? I managed to finish high school and got a job as a carhop and I married Joe Carr before I was eighteen. He was only twenty-one, and I must have been out of my mind because it couldn't have been worse. He was a runner for a bookie and when he had been drinking—sometimes I think he worked out on me just to keep in practice—he had to prove how tough he was. He was arrested twice for assault in one year and the second time I got a divorce.

"I never saw him after that," she said. "Which was the one good break I had. I worked in San Diego for a while, but I always wanted to get into the movies—most girls out there do who aren't downright homely—and I came back to Hollywood again. After I'd registered I did get a few jobs as an extra and I was working as a waitress in a place where I could get time off when anything came up. I got to meet a few people and one, a sort of assistant assistant director, finally got me a screen test. I guess the test was all right," she said, "but I couldn't act. They told me to get some experience and come back again, so I started working with a little theater group. . . . Didn't George ever tell you any of this?" she asked abruptly.

"All he said was that you'd been married before and that you and another girl came east on a bus," Murdock said.

"That's right," she said, and chuckled softly, as though remembering some long-forgotten incident that was amusing. "A director down at Laguna said he could get us a summer job in Maine if we could find a way to get east, so we came. And that was the summer George had his boat up there for a month and after I met him I didn't want to be an actress any more. I never thought it could happen after I met Harriett—she never did like me; she thinks I'm common—but George was in love with me."

"Yes," Murdock said. "He was."

He watched her finish her drink and put the glass aside, knowing what Harriett meant but not agreeing with her. There was something about the girl that told him that she had not been born a lady. She lacked the grace and brittleness of those who had been moulded by wealth and position and the proper finishing schools. Both her background and her education left something to be desired and there were times when she seemed unsure of herself, but she was not common by Murdock's standards.

The word that came to him was young. Even though she was twenty-four and had more experience in some phases of life than most women ever have, she still seemed young to him; young and vital and friendly and trying very hard since her marriage to live down the rough edges of her past. It was one of the reasons why he liked her and what he said next did not come easy.

"I don't think George ever knew it but you didn't really love him, did you?"

She looked right at him then, her lips parted and her eyes bewildered. That she answered honestly was probably due to her inability to contain her surprise.

"How did you know?" she asked in a voice he could hardly hear. "I thought I did when I married him," she said when he did not reply. "Really I did. I'd never known anyone quite like him. I couldn't believe anyone like that would ever want to marry me. I was sure I did."

She frowned and her tone grew indignant. "I did love him in a way," she said, "because he was kind and good and fun to be with. I did the things he liked. I knew how to please him. I was a good wife and I made him happy."

"Yes," Murdock said. "I think you did. The only reason I mentioned it at all is because I'm wondering what you're going to do about Jerry."

"What about Jerry?" she asked, her glance suddenly narrowing.

"He was in love with you before the accident, wasn't he?"

She stood up suddenly, knocking over her glass. She picked it up and banged it on the table. She took three aimless steps, turned, and came back.

"What kind of talk is that?" she demanded, her voice shrill. "Just what do you mean?"

Murdock eyed her steadily, waiting, the feeling growing that he had been right. He could not tell her why he was interested in Jerry, but he had to find out what he could while he could.

"I don't blame you for being sore," he said. "I'll take off if you say so. I don't think you were ever disloyal to George," he said. "I don't think Jerry could have got to first base so long as you were married. But I used to notice how he'd look at you and I think he's jealous now. I think he's worried about you and your half brother."

"Barry?" Her eyes opened again and were suddenly uncertain as she sat down on the chaise. "Why?"

Murdock went on quickly as her resentment evaporated. "Brady was interested in Barry too," he said. "He phoned Kirby from San Francisco and asked Kirby to do some checking." He paused and said: "Kirby says Denham hasn't turned a wheel in the last three weeks and yet he always has money to go to the track and spend his nights at the Club Saville."

"What about it?"

"Kirby says you've been seeing Denham pretty often—going to his hotel and having dinner with him."

"Why shouldn't I?" she flared. "He's my half brother."

"Jerry's been watching him too. He knows about those times you've been with him," Murdock said, stretching the truth a bit. "And why should Jerry do that unless he's jealous? Why should he be jealous unless he's in love with you?"

She rose again, her mouth stiff and the look in her eyes warning Murdock that he had about come to the end of the interview.

"And suppose he is?" she said. "What's wrong with that? Haven't you ever heard of men marrying the widows of their brothers' or best friends'—or the other way around? Is that so awful?"

Murdock agreed that it was not. He said he knew of such marriages and all of them had turned out well, possibly because both partners knew exactly what they were getting.

"I just wanted to get things straight in my mind," he said. And then, as an afterthought: "If Jerry wanted to marry you he'd have to get his mother's permission, wouldn't he? Isn't that the way his father's will read? I mean if he expects to inherit anything."

"We could wait," she said. "The doctors have told Harriett she hasn't more than two years to live and probably a lot less."

"All right, Rita," he said, aware that in this instance she spoke the truth. "And you're sure you never knew anyone named Ruth Colby out in California?"

"Never."

"Or Benjamin Danton?"

"No."

"But you were married in Los Angeles."

"I told you I was."

"And where did you get your divorce?"

For just an instant there seemed to be a break in the self-contained assurance that had been both stubborn and defiant. Then she said: "The same place, why?"

Murdock did not answer that one but turned and went down the stairs, his dissatisfaction growing as he descended. Yet, by the time he had reached the sidewalk, he knew that his time had not been wasted. He had learned some things he had heretofore only suspected; the only trouble was that there was no way of knowing how much of what had been said was the truth and how much was not.

His car was parked across the street and he sat in it a moment, too occupied with his thoughts to press the starter. That was how he happened to notice the taxi stop in front of the Aldersons. When he saw Gloria get out and pay the driver he knew what he wanted to do.

A drugstore on Newbury Street provided a telephone booth, and when Henderson's soft voice came to him he identified himself and asked if he could speak to Mrs. Donald Alderson. She came on the wire almost at once and he asked her if she could meet him somewhere for a drink. He said she could name the time and place, adding that he thought it was important.

"I'm afraid not, Kent," she said. "The only thing that's important to me now is a hot tub."

"You've got plenty of time," Murdock said. "You can still make the Ritz bar by five, and then we can talk about that Florida trip you took this spring."

That brought on a long moment of silence. When the reply came there was a subtle change in the tone.

"Was your detective friend in Florida?"

"He just came from there."

"All right," she said. "It may be that I'll need a drink. I'll try to make it by five."

12

MURDOCK was sitting at the bar nursing his first drink when Gloria Alderson came through the doorway. She saw him as he slid off his stool and he went to meet her, guiding her to a table next to the wall and asking if this would be all right.

When he had ordered her Scotch-and-soda he took a moment to study her and it came to him then that she and Rita had very little in common. For there was nothing unsure about Gloria. Even seeing her across the room two things would be at once apparent to most men: that she was a striking-looking woman with an exceptional figure, and that she was also expensive. It was not so much the quality of her clothes, which had been fashioned by experts—in the casual manner this time, with a pastel-green dress and a cashmere coat—or the size of her engagement ring or the sapphire-and-diamond cocktail ring on her little finger; rather it was the way she carried herself and the manner with which her green eyes considered her surroundings. Perhaps because she came from the South there was a languorous quality about her that was at once apparent, but when Murdock examined the eyes and the shape of the generous mouth with its short upper lip, he

knew there was some hidden vitality here that could make
her a passionate woman when aroused.

"Well"—she lifted her glass, her glance amused—"shall
we start the inquisition? What's this about my Florida
trip?"

Murdock gave her a prologue similar to the one he had
given her sister-in-law, but from then on he had to bluff.
The copies of the two hotel cards he had photographed
for Brady had told him nothing but the names, and because he was not sure about the dates, he had to guess.

"You and Arthur Enders were at the same Miami Beach
hotel at the same time," he said. "Was that coincidence?"

"Hardly." The small gleam of amusement remained and
there was no embarrassment in her accented tone. "Arthur
knew where I was going to be and he thought it might be
fun to spend some time at the same hotel. . . . Why?" she
asked calmly. "Does it prove anything? I mean, there were
plenty of unattached men around; there always are.

"Can I help it," she asked, "if Donald refuses to take
me? I don't propose to spend fifty-two weeks a year under
Harriett's watchful and disapproving eye. I have to get
away, and I mean literally, or I'd go crazy. I told Donald
so. I used to beg him to go with me but it's never done
much good. Business, he says, though I have an idea that
it's as much his mother as business. So when things get
too difficult around the house I announce my plans and
Donald is very sweet about it. He's sorry he can't go just
then but he knows the trip will do me good, and have a
good time and be sure to write."

She tipped her head. "So that's the way it's been the last
year or so, and when I take a trip you don't think I live like
a nun, do you? There's always some man to take you to
dinner or to the races; to dance with you or just lie on the

beach. If I wanted to cheat—I mean, if that's what I had in mind—I wouldn't have to wait for Arthur. The advantage of being alone is that you can accept an invitation or not, as you like. Arthur's fun. He does things well. I like him. Does that answer your question?"

Murdock had not been prepared for such frankness but he took it in stride. He grinned back at her, his dark eyes steady.

"You make it sound good," he said, "but you're over-simplifying, aren't you?"

"How do you mean?"

"You say you had fun and nothing more, but divorces have been granted on less evidence than Tom Brady had in those two signature cards. Did Donald know Enders was with you all that time? Did his mother? If you *had* been sleeping with him, would you be likely to admit it?"

Her smile went away and her voice grew petulant. "If I didn't know you I'd say this was a prelude to blackmail."

"Then let me carry it a step further." Murdock pushed his glass aside. "Because George was a friend of mine I happen to know a little about his father's will. As you know, he made bequests to all three sons but he showed a lot of favoritism, maybe because George was the one who really put the family business on its feet. George was the one who saw the possibilities of this do-it-yourself move-ment and he climbed aboard by converting about half the production from the heavy power tools Alderson had al-ways made to smaller and less expensive merchandise.

"Whatever the reason, Donald was left twenty-five thou-sand outright and Jerry got the same. George got a hun-dred and fifty thousand. The rest of it went to Harriett, in trust for the sons, but still with some power of veto, so with George gone Donald and Jerry stand to split the remainder—if they keep on the right side of Harriett. That much I know," he said. "And now I'm going to guess. You can stop me if I'm wrong, but I don't think there's much left between you and Donald. . . . Was there ever?" he asked when she hesitated.

"Yes. There might still be if Donald ever asserted himself and got out from under his mother's thumb. I married him because I thought I loved him, and for a while we were happy. I know that. I'm not going to tell you that I didn't know that he came from a well-to-do family or that money didn't influence me because it wouldn't be true. I had to marry a man with means. My parents knew it and I knew it."

She hesitated while she drew a circle on the table with the bottom of her glass. "Luckily I was the only daughter and what money we had for clothes went to me. We had the social position and the name in our town, and all the time I was growing up and going to the right schools the house was falling apart inside because my father was an incompetent gentleman. If I told you how many times I was the belle of the ball at college proms you wouldn't believe me, and then all of a sudden I discovered it was getting very late. I was twenty-seven when I married Don. I never regretted it, though I must admit that your guess about the present arrangement is close. There's not much left. He's afraid of his mother. For myself, I'm getting tired of a semi-platonic marriage. I want something more; I'm still not too old to have a family." She glanced up. "But my tastes are much too expensive to chuck it all now."

"What about Enders?"

"What about him? I like him. He has a way of treating women that is flattering. But he tried it with two wives without much success and I'm not sure I could do any better. I'm not in love with him, if that's what you mean. At least not now."

"You're going to stay with Donald until he gets his half of the estate," Murdock said, "and that's what makes those hotel cards important."

"Look," she said, her exasperation showing. "I don't follow you, but if there's going to be much of this I'd like another drink, please."

Murdock said he was sorry and caught the waiter's eye.

"Just what is it you're after?" she said when the man withdrew.

"A motive for murder."

"And you think I have one?"

"Well, what happens if Donald decides your stay with Enders was something more than fun and games? What if his mother says it's time for a divorce?"

She watched the waiter put down the drinks. "I suppose things might get rather sticky."

"You'd hardly be in a position to do much bargaining."

"Bargaining?"

"About alimony, or a settlement."

"I wouldn't know about that."

Murdock realized that there was not much more he could say. At the moment he did not think she had killed Brady, but he wanted to do something to jar her complacency.

"The police know that a woman was looking for Brady's office about the time he was killed," he said.

He watched the trim brows climb, but nothing changed in her manner or in her voice.

"Oh?"

"She was wearing a camel's-hair coat."

She glanced down at her own coat. "I'm afraid this is as close as I can come to camel's-hair," she said.

"A tallish woman."

"Well, that much applies."

"You haven't any alibi, and neither has Enders. I wonder how much he'd stand to lose if Harriett decided to change lawyers."

He put his glass down as he spoke and now he saw her glance fix beyond him and quickly brighten with a smile. "Why don't you ask him?" she said. "Hello, Arthur. We were just talking about you."

By the time Murdock looked round Arthur Enders had come to a stop beside him, and now he rose and said hello. He asked if Enders would join them and what would he have. Enders had never been more gracious. He was wearing a flannel suit that was a shade lighter than navy, a white Oxford shirt and a regimental-striped tie. His graying hair had been carefully combed, his voice was friendly and his tanned face wore his smile well. Only the eyes seemed wary as he said Scotch would do very nicely.

"Black Label," he said to the waiter. "With Perrier, if you please."

"Kent is looking for motives for murder," Gloria said. "He was just asking about you."

"Really?" said Enders, sounding as though he could not care less. "Did he make any accusations?"

"He says that Mr. Brady found out we were at the same hotel at the same time," she said, and then she was repeating some of the things Murdock had told her.

Enders listened politely as he sipped his drink. For the most part he gave his attention to the woman, and when he did look at Murdock he seemed at ease, hanging on to his smile in spite of the calculating glint in his eyes.

"I wouldn't worry about it," he said when she finished. "Harriett's a practical woman. . . . Though I admit your information has some nuisance value," he said to Murdock. "Was there anything else?"

Murdock had already signaled for the check and now he put a bill on the tray. He knew there was no point in continuing to talk to Enders and he wondered if Gloria had telephoned the lawyer to inform him of this appointment. He had an idea Enders's appearance was planned and now, as he pushed back his chair and made his excuses, he recalled some of the things Frank Kirby had said about the lawyer's financial status.

Seeing him now and remembering his background and training, he did not look like a candidate for murder and yet the motive was there. For the management of the Alderson estate must provide a tidy income; in addition Enders had been appointed administrator of George Alderson's estate when it was discovered that George had died intestate. Enders would make his accounting shortly and he alone would say how much would be left for Rita. It was pointless now to speculate as to the possibility of Enders using funds that were not his own, but it seemed to Murdock that such a man might kill if his way of life was about to be destroyed and his future ruined. Now, as he stood up, Enders rose with him.

"This information of yours," he said. "Is it something that you got from Brady?"

"Indirectly."

"The police have the same information?"

"I doubt it."

"But you propose to tell them."

"I don't know," Murdock said, and at the moment this was the truth.

Then, deciding that he had no obligation to amplify the statement, he nodded to Gloria and heard her thank him for the drinks. As he glanced back from the doorway he saw that Enders was still on his feet.

13

IT WAS nearly six thirty when Murdock walked into the lobby of the Clay Hotel and angled toward the house telephones. Barry Denham answered almost at once, telling him to come up, and a minute or so later Murdock was in a fourth-floor room that had a disordered look and smelled strongly of shaving lotion and toilet water.

Denham was clad in light-gray slacks and a blue shirt. His head was wet and shiny, and as Murdock closed the door Denham stood in front of a mirror and began the ritual of combing the long black hair. This took quite a while and was done with great care, Denham's big body hunched a little so he could see what he was doing, his head turned slightly from side to side as the proper effect was achieved.

"What's new?" he said. "Throw that towel into the bathroom and sit down. Give me a minute and I'll buy a drink."

Murdock picked up the wadded bath towel and tossed it through the open door. He sat down on the chair, unbuttoning his jacket and reaching for his cigarettes, fascinated now by Denham's technique and watching him put the comb down and begin to work on the sides of his head above the close-set ears with delicate strokes of the brush.

"You want to get a couple of glasses?" he said.

"I'll get one for you," Murdock said.

"What's the matter," Denham said, still studying himself. "You on the wagon or something?"

Murdock brought a glass from the bathroom. He said he had just finished two drinks and that was enough for now.

"I was talking to your sister this afternoon," he said.

"Yeah? What about?"

"I've been trying to find out what Tom Brady was doing in California and why he was interested in two birth certificates. I thought maybe she might know one of the names."

"What names?"

"Ruth Colby and Benjamin Danton."

"Did she?"

"No."

"Neither do I." Denham, satisfied at last with his handiwork, put down the brush and took a bottle of Bourbon from a drawer. "Sure you won't change your mind?" he said and poured his drink.

"Did you see much of Rita out there?" Murdock asked.

"Not the past few years. I left home before she did. We kept in touch. You know, maybe I'd get a letter once or twice a year. She got herself married to some crumb and had to get rid of him and I was drifting around here and there."

"Were you always an actor?"

"Hell, no." Denham grinned and tasted the whisky. "I was in the army and worked in an aircraft factory for a while. But I was going with this girl, see, and she was a dancer. We used to go to the Palladium two or three times a week and she kept telling me how wonderful I was and why didn't I take it up seriously. Well, she had a friend who was a teacher; you know, had a studio, and she wouldn't give up until I went to see him."

He chuckled and reached for a necktie that reminded Murdock of a bouquet of spring flowers.

"And you know something," he said. "She was right. I was pretty good. Inside of six months I was getting a little work in the studios. You know, sort of a chorus boy in musicals; things like that. And brother, they've got some real cute numbers out there too. I didn't get interested in the acting part until later. A dress extra first and then a bit here and there. I was in Mexico with a company when Rita wrote and told me about her husband. She said this neck of the woods was lousy with summer theaters, so why didn't I come and see what I could do."

"You haven't found anything, have you?"

"Not definite."

"Have you looked?"

Denham turned from the mirror, brows bunching. "What do you mean by that?"

"Brady hired Frank Kirby to keep an eye on you. Kirby says you've been too busy at the track to look for a job."

"Wait a minute." Denham's mouth tightened and the little mustache seemed to spread. "You mean Kirby's been tailin' me?"

"Part of the time."

"What the hell for?"

Murdock gestured with one hand. He said he did not know. He said he was not sure Brady had told Kirby why he wanted Denham followed.

"Kirby says someone else has been keeping an eye on you," he said.

"Who?"

"Jerry Alderson." Murdock waited. So did Denham, his

eyes mean. "I think he's in love with your sister," Murdock
said.

Denham turned away and suddenly his voice was in-
different.

"Seems like a nice guy," he said, and went over to pick
up his jacket which lay on the bed.

"But you don't know any reason why Brady should want
you followed?"

Denham put on his coat, which was a brown tweed with
a flashy pattern and padded shoulders. When he had fixed
the handkerchief in the breast pocket the way he wanted
it he said:

"Do you?"

"All I know is that you come from California and that
Brady was in California. He must have found out something about you that interested him—or Mrs. Alderson—
or he wouldn't have called long distance to hire Kirby.
Just how much Kirby knows I'm not sure."

"That makes us even." Denham went over to the chest
to take the last swallow of whisky and then glanced at his
watch. "Sorry, pal," he said, "but I've got to get going."

Kent Murdock ate his dinner in the downstairs grill—
lamb chops, a baked potato, and a green salad—not because he particularly liked the place but because it was
handy. When he sat down he did not think he was hungry
but an extra-dry martini helped and he ate everything. It
was while he was having coffee that he began to think
about Walt Carey, and when he left the hotel he did not
bother to telephone but drove directly to the hospital.

Carey was sitting up in bed, scowling unhappily and
looking strangely out of place in the white hospital
jacket. His face had a scrubbed look and his graying hair

was neatly combed and the reason for his current state of melancholia became at once apparent when he saw Murdock.

"My God, am I glad to see you," he said. "You haven't got a drink on you, have you?"

Murdock laughed aloud and pulled a chair up to the bed. "No," he said. "How do you feel?"

"Terrible."

"Does your head ache?"

"No. Not now. It ain't that. I just need a drink. . . . Look," he said, his glance scheming and his voice a conspirator's whisper. "You could go out and sneak me in a pint, couldn't you?"

"No."

"A half pint?" Hopefully.

"What's the doctor say? He could prescribe a drink."

Carey's opinion of the doctor was profane and somewhat lengthy.

"He says I can go home tomorrow and if I want to drink then it's okay with him, but while he's responsible for me, no drink."

Murdock chuckled again because he could not help it, and Carey bristled.

"What's so damn funny?"

"You are. I can't get used to seeing you without that silly cap."

"Yeah," said Carey. "The Doc says if it hadn't been for that silly cap I could've got a cracked skull. . . . Say, I'm sorry about the films."

"Forget it," Murdock said. "Did you get a look at the guy? How did it happen?"

The story Carey told was simple enough, his own part in the action completely understandable to anyone who knew him. For over the years Carey had demonstrated a courage that often approached the foolhardy, and he was particularly resentful of anyone who interfered with his work or attempted to meddle with his camera or equipment. That he was on the small side physically had never made any difference. Now he said that he had seen the man who had slugged him.

"You know there's not much light in that printing room and I don't think I ever saw him before, but if they've got a halfway decent mug shot of him down at Headquarters I can pick it out. . . . A big guy," he said. "Sort of blond with a broad face and big ears."

"Where was he?"

"I was coming out with the films and I saw him standing there in the outer room as I came along the hall. I didn't pay any attention to him, thought he might be waiting for someone. Before I knew it he was right behind me. I shifted the film clips to my left hand, between the fingers, and asked him what he wanted.

"He said, 'Are those the pictures you brought back from Kelleher's?' and I said, 'Yeah. Why?' 'I'll take 'em,' he said, and I said, 'Like hell you will.'

"I told him to shove off and not bother me and he reached for the films. When I saw he meant it I swung at him. Hit him pretty good too, but a little high, and he had a head like a rock. He had me by the wrist then, the one that had the films, and all I could do was swing again and I think he must have spun me around. But I don't know. I don't remember a thing. Not getting hit, not anything until I wake up here in the sack with a headache."

Murdock thought it over, his hunch that the attempt had nothing to do with Brady's murder confirmed. He asked if the police had been here to talk to Carey.

"Lieutenant Walsh was in," Carey said. "I'm sorry about the films. If I hadn't—"

"I said forget it," Murdock said. "You never should have tried to take the fellow."

"Hell, he probably would have slugged me anyway," Carey said. "He couldn't just walk out with them, could he? I'd be tagging along and screaming my head off, wouldn't I? And anyway those aren't the films I meant. I mean the ones you told me to put in the envelope when they were dry."

Murdock sat up slowly, his dark gaze suddenly intent and his interest quickening as his mind began to race.

"What about them?"

"Nothing, except I didn't get a chance to do what you said. Right after you went out this call came about the holdup in Cambridge and there wasn't anybody else within five miles of the place. I had to go."

"So where are they?" Murdock said, still afraid to hope.

"Right where you left 'em."

"Hanging there drying?"

"Yeah. I was going to take care of 'em when I dumped the new batch in the tank but I never got the chance."

What Carey said after that was lost to Murdock because he was too busy trying to recall each little detail of the night before, to remember just what he had done when he had found Carey unconscious. Only then was he certain that he had not once thought to look at the drying wires and see if the films were there. Assuming that Carey had already taken care of them hours earlier, he had not even gone back to the printing room after the doctor arrived. Now, coming to his feet, he could feel his pulse accelerating as new hope came to him.

He told Carey to be a good boy and take care of himself.

He said he would buy Carey a few drinks tomorrow to make up for the one he could not supply at the moment.

"You got a customer," Carey said. "I accept."

Then Murdock was in the hall, hurrying a little now as he walked to the elevator, and the impatience began to build inside him.

14

KENT MURDOCK was still hurrying when he came into the studio anteroom a little after nine. A glance at his office told him it was open but empty and when he saw that Estey was on hand at the long desk to take care of any calls, he went on into the printing room without slowing down. He was a little out of breath now, though this may have been due more to his inner excitement than to the physical effort he had expended, and without even bothering to look at the films then drying on the wires, he turned at once to the open-faced cabinet on his left.

This was a homemade file a little higher than his head and perhaps three feet wide, the interior made up of box-like compartments, each of which was numbered with a day of the month. It served as a perpetual one-month file of all the negatives that had been taken by the staff and it was the duty of the office boy to collect each day's films, put them in the proper compartment, and remove the ones which had been put there a month earlier on that date. Anything older than that was considered to be of no value.

Taking the handful of negatives that had been filed late last night or early that morning, Murdock began to examine them under the light and the second one he looked at told him that the routine of the department had functioned perfectly.

For what he saw was a photograph of a birth certificate and he told himself that if one of the negatives he had made for Brady was here, they all were. Then, with the pressure lifting and his breathing more regular, he relaxed and took his time sorting out the remaining negatives, making two piles and then counting the ones that interested him. There were fourteen of these, just as he remembered, and he understood that coincidence in the form of a rush assignment for Walt Carey had perhaps preserved the evidence that Brady had worked so hard to accumulate.

On the heels of this thought came another that sobered him. Here, if one knew how to put them together, were bits and pieces of information that might substitute for the reports that were stolen from Brady's office. Brady, in his wish to preserve certain facts, had taken the precaution to have them photographed and it occurred to Murdock that it would be both ironic and just if his friend's foresight could now serve to trap the one who had killed him.

He still had the negatives in his hand as he came back to the anteroom and although he knew that he must make prints before he could tell just what he had, he was no longer in a hurry and he had already decided that it would be better to do the work in the privacy of his own apartment. As he moved toward his office to get an envelope, Estey looked up.

"Oh, Kent," he said. "I almost forgot. A fellow named Frank Kirby was looking for you. He said he'd be back."

Murdock said all right and turned on the light in his cubby. He put the films in an envelope and tucked it into an inside pocket. He glanced over the assignment book

from sheer force of habit and saw that all current nota-
tions had been crossed off. He called the city room to see
if everything was all right and the night city editor told
him it looked like a quiet evening. It was when he lit a
cigarette and leaned back in his chair to rest and think a
moment about his discovery that Frank Kirby appeared in
the doorway.

Kirby was chewing gum, his jaw muscles bulging with
the effort. His gray-green eyes were busy as always as they
scanned the room and returned to Murdock, and now he
pushed back his light-gray hat and loosened the button on
his double-breasted jacket.

"I've been looking for you," he said.

"So Estey said."

"I began to wonder if you still worked here."

"I'm taking a couple of days off," Murdock said. "I was
over to see Walt Carey," he added. "He got a look at the
fellow who slugged him but he doesn't remember seeing
him before."

"Does it hook up with Brady?"

"I don't think so."

Kirby nodded thoughtfully and let his jaws rest.
"Where're you going now?"

"Home."

"I could use a ride," Kirby said. "My car's in the shop.
If you've done any good for yourself you could come up
and have a drink and tell me about it."

"Okay." Murdock stood up and snapped off the light.
When he had called to tell Estey he would not be back, he
led the way from the room.

Frank Kirby lived in an old four-story brick apartment
just off Charles Street. Murdock had never been there be-

fore and when he parked he let Kirby lead the way through
a ground-floor vestibule that had two rows of mailboxes on
one wall and a collapsible baby carriage tucked in one corner. Kirby said they would have to climb a bit, and as Murdock went up the stairs he saw that there were four
apartments to a floor, two on either side of a hall that ran
from front to rear.

"One more," Kirby said as they started up the third flight
and then he began to swear softly. "The damn light's out
again," he said, and now Murdock realized the hall above
lay in darkness except for the reflected light that came from
above and below.

Music from a radio or television set was blasting from a
near-by door, but he could hear Kirby take out his keys,
turning right into the shadowed corridor and angling toward the door across the hall. Murdock was perhaps two
steps behind him, still closer to the wall on his right than
the one Kirby approached, when it happened.

Murdock heard the key click in the lock and the knob
turn, and then the hall seemed to explode with sound and
from the far corner of his eye he saw the flash of light erupt
and then erupt again.

That Murdock moved at all was due to an involuntary
muscular spasm over which he had no control. In the con-
fines of the narrow hall the first shot sounded like a cannon
and he jumped, feeling the wall at his back and then, realizing what must have happened, trying to flatten against
it as the second shot crashed and reverberated along the
hall.

Only vaguely could he see Kirby at the door, but with
the second shot—perhaps before that—he saw the detective
go down. He heard him hit the floor and now, his heart
in his throat and remembering the window at the rear of

the floor below, he understood that they had been fired at
from a similar window, though he could not yet locate it.
All he knew was that he had not been hit, that he was just
beginning to get scared as he waited unconsciously for another shot.

When none came and he heard the rattle of some metallic sound beyond the open window, he seemed to know
that the unseen gunman had fled; it was then that he
started for the shadowy figure on the floor, breath held and
his heart beginning to pound.

"Kirby!" he yelled, his voice ragged. "Are you hit?"

He knew an instant later that Kirby was all right. For
Kirby had jumped to his feet and wheeled into the hall,
cursing now in a soft vicious monotone as he started for
the rear window.

Murdock followed, still a bit shaken but feeling immeas-
urably better. He saw the window was open and he waited
there while Kirby leaned far out. Beyond he could make
out the spidery outline of a fire escape but he made no
attempt to push Kirby aside. Seconds later the detective
pulled his head back and lowered the window, his cursing
dwindling to a persistent guttural muttering that was
partly lost in the background of the television set that was
still blasting. Then, up ahead, a door opened and light
spilled into the hall to reveal the silhouette of a man in
pajamas and bathrobe.

"Who's that?" he demanded. "What's the trouble out
here?"

"It's Frank Kirby, Mr. Bronson," Kirby said. "It's okay
now."

"I thought I heard somebody shooting."

"You did. Some prowler on the fire escape. I guess he was

afraid we'd grab him, so he threw a couple of shots toward us to keep us away."

A woman in a quilted wrap and her hair in curlers appeared at her husband's shoulder to say she did not know what the world was coming to.

"A body's not safe in his own home any more. You ought to call the police."

"I'm going to, Mrs. Bronson," Kirby said. "You just stay there and lock the door and then you won't get mixed up in it."

He turned away, moved inside his own apartment, and snapped on a light. Waiting until the Bronsons' door closed, he got a flashlight and began to examine the walls and casing.

"Who was he shooting at?" Murdock said.

"Not you, pal."

"I just froze there," Murdock said. "When I heard you fall it scared hell out of me."

"I didn't fall," Kirby said. "I took a dive. I learned that much in the war. I heard the first slug hit and down I went. . . . Yeah," he said, and focused the beam of the flashlight on the edge of the casing. "Right here."

He pointed to the small hole in the woodwork, a clean round hole that was barely noticeable because the bullet had gone straight in.

"The other one must be down the hall somewhere," he said. "But the hell with it. Come on."

He motioned Murdock into the room, closed the door, and went over to the telephone. He dialed a number and asked some questions and when he hung up he said:

"Bacon's not in. I could call the precinct but—" He let the sentence hang there and spoke of something else. "What's the point?" he said. "That was no prowler. That guy had murder on his mind. He was planted on the fire escape and he probably unscrewed the light bulb. He was a pretty fair shot too. If I'd been alone—"

He turned abruptly, went along an inner hall and into another room, turning on lights as he moved. When he came back he had a shoulder holster in one hand and a short-barreled revolver in the other. Placing the holster on a table, he flipped the cylinder from the gun with a practiced gesture, spun it to be sure it was loaded, and clicked it back into place.

"From now on," he said, "maybe I'd better pack this with me. How about the drink? You can get the ice."

He led the way into the kitchen and while Murdock pried ice from a tray, Kirby opened a cupboard and brought out Scotch, Bourbon, and a bottle of soda.

"Pour your own," he said. "Make it a good one. Soda or water?"

They took their drinks into the living room and Murdock saw that it was comfortably furnished in an ordinary sort of way. The chairs and the davenport looked used but there was no sign of ostentation and the only thing lacking was something on the walls. There were no pictures or prints, but apparently Kirby had a blind spot in this respect and did not miss them.

Now he took off his double-breasted jacket, draped it neatly on the back of a straight-backed chair. He dropped his gum in the wastebasket, took a long pull on his drink, and eased into a club chair, his legs extended. When he was ready he fixed his gray-green eyes on Murdock, the upward-slanting brows slightly bunched over his nose and his hard jaw set so that his lips did not move much when he spoke.

"He wasn't after you," he said. "Not if it's the same guy

you ran into in Brady's place last night. That time he could have dropped you. He didn't. He just let one shot go when it looked like you were going to follow him into the alley. This was different."

Murdock nodded, his mind busy as he recalled Kirby's reputation. "Who have you been getting tough with?"

"I don't know," Kirby said, and sounded as if he meant it.

"What about the two that came to my place last night? You were going to check on them."

"I know who they are. One's a bouncer and the other's a spare-time bartender in a joint on Columbus Avenue."

"Who owns it?"

Kirby mentioned a name that meant nothing to Murdock. "But that guy's only the owner of record," he said. "Could be someone behind him who did the hiring." His frown bit deeper. "But somehow they don't figure on a caper like this. From what I know about them they're too small time."

Murdock lit a cigarette and considered the statement. "But assuming this has something to do with Brady, who've you got? You can hardly figure a woman."

"Hardly," Kirby said, "but you can't rule it out."

"That leaves Enders and Jerry Alderson, his brother Donald, and Barry Denham. I've known Donald quite a while," Murdock said. "He's the sort you'd think would be afraid to pick up a gun."

"Okay," Kirby said. "A lot of people have been killed by the same kind of guys. You figure they wouldn't hurt a fly. Milquetoasts. Sunday-school characters. Until one fine day they blow their top. If Donald Alderson killed Brady— maybe not intending to when he went there—he's already been initiated. He could kill again if he had to."

Such reasoning was sound and Murdock knew it. He had

been on the *Courier* too long to rule out such possibilities
and he realized now that he was letting personal consid-
erations take the place of logic. Because he knew the Aldersons it was hard for him to imagine that they—or any of
their friends—could be guilty of murder, and from a practical standpoint such reasoning was specious.

"And anyway," Kirby said, "they could hire somebody,
couldn't they? Especially Enders. He's a lawyer; he knows
people. If his own neck was in danger he could find someone to come up here with a gun, and you know it. . . .
I've been doing some checking on Jerry," he said, "but I
don't think he knows it. . . . And that Denham—he could
be a bad one.

"I called the coast," he continued. "I know a couple of
guys out there—agency guys—and they're going to see
what they can find out about Denham, if anything. But
that'll probably take a couple of days, so how do you figure
it? Who've you been talking to?"

Murdock told him what he had done that afternoon and
when he finished, Kirby was scowling, not so much from
annoyance, it seemed, but from his own nervous impatience.

"I don't get it," he said finally. "If any one of them was
guilty you don't think they'd admit it, do you? What were
you trying to prove?"

"I'm trying to get the family set-up," Murdock said,
studying the end of his cigarette as he considered the films
in his pocket and deciding to say nothing about them until he'd had a chance to know exactly what each one of
them meant. "I noticed a couple of things when I made
those photographs for Brady," he said. "Not too much because I tried not to get too curious. But what little I did see
opens up some motives."

He took a breath and said: "I'm not going to try to tell you all the details because some of them are probably unimportant, but I saw enough to get the idea that every one of those people might—and I mean might—stand a chance to lose important money if Harriett Alderson got her hands on Brady's reports and she made up her mind to get tough with them. She holds most of the purse strings."

"She calls the shots," Kirby said. "Have you told Bacon?"

"No. Because what little I know isn't enough. It's not evidence and it could cause trouble for some innocent people."

"You're getting sort of choosy," Kirby said bluntly. "Brady was a friend of yours. I thought that was why—"

"I'm not going to pop off until I know more than I do now," Murdock said stubbornly. Then because he did not want to argue, he said: "How about you? Did you do any good this afternoon?"

"Maybe. Did Bacon tell you about the tenant who saw the dame in the lobby last night? The one that was looking for Brady's office."

"Yes."

"Well, I think I saw her."

Murdock sat up slowly. He put his glass aside. "You mean, you know who she is?"

"No."

"But—"

"I said I thought I *saw* her. . . . Last night."

"Maybe you forgot to mention it," Murdock said.

"I told you how it was with me this noon." Kirby's gaze remained steady but his mouth was crooked with an incipient grin. "If I can help the police you put my name in the paper. So I'm waiting until I see if I can do any good. You help me; I help you, but for now this is between the two of us, okay?"

Murdock nodded, a picture growing in his mind of the girl Bacon had described that morning.

"It was about nine," Kirby said. "A little after because it had started to rain and that's how I happened to see her. I'd just come around the corner when it started to pour and I ducked into a doorway. I lit a cigarette and waited, hoping it might slack up in a couple of minutes. I was still there when I saw her in the doorway. You couldn't say I got a real good look at her because there's not much light in the lobby and besides it was raining.

"But from where I stood," he said, "she looked taller than most dames—like Bacon's tenant said. And the coat looked like it could be camel's-hair and she was wearing a scarf. About the dark glasses I'm not sure even now. But one thing, she was in a hurry. She sort of stepped back when she saw it was raining and then she started out, half-running toward the corner across from me. . . . Also," he said, "she was carrying a pretty good-sized bag. I noticed that much and I thought it was one of those shoulder bags you see. Now I'm thinking maybe it could have been a brief-case."

"She didn't have a car?"

"If she did it was parked around the corner. It would have been a cinch for me if I'd had any idea of what had happened. I didn't, and now I'm hoping she didn't have a car. If she took a cab there's a chance I can find the driver. It's going to be tough but I'm working on it. That's another reason I'm holding out on Bacon. If I can find out who it was and dump it in his lap—" He broke off and shrugged. "Well, it might help."

Murdock sat where he was a silent moment, finding

nothing he wanted to say. When he noticed his glass and saw that it was not yet empty, he finished his drink. He pulled himself slowly out of his chair.

"It's a better lead than I've got," he said.

"If it works out," Kirby said. "The good ones sometimes don't. I'll keep in touch," he said. "Maybe I'll get something on Denham."

He started across the room with Murdock and then he stopped in the little entryway to open a closet door. "Wait a minute," he said, and took a raincoat from a hanger. "Is this yours?"

Murdock took it and glanced at the label. He said yes, and asked where Kirby got it.

"The only way I can figure it is that that stupid butler at Aldersons' handed out the wrong coats last night. I didn't put mine on—it wasn't raining then."

"Neither did I," Murdock said, remembering how he had tossed his coat into the back of the car.

"I didn't notice it until I started to hang it up," Kirby said, "and somehow it didn't look quite right. When I saw the Brooks label I knew damn well it wasn't mine. . . . Take it along," he said. "I'll pick mine up sometime or maybe you could take it to your office if you think of it; I can stop by tomorrow."

Murdock opened the door, his glance moving once more to the bullet hole. "What about this?"

"Bacon'll probably want to have somebody dig it out," Kirby said. "I'll tell him. You never know. It could be important." He grunted softly and his voice thinned out. "One thing: this guy tries it again and old Kirby's gonna shoot back."

15

WITH HIS landlord's permission Kent Murdock had made a few changes in his apartment during the years he had lived there, and one of the most important to him was his darkroom. Originally a dinette adjoining the kitchen, it was just the right size for his needs, and by adding two doors, some additional plumbing, and a special shade for the one window, he had made a self-contained and light-proof unit that was both compact and efficient.

Now, at twenty minutes after ten, he had his jacket off and his preparations made. The heat had been turned on in the small ferrotyper, he had the proper paper at hand, and he had adjusted his enlarger and easel to accommodate an eleven-by-fourteen print. Without stopping to sort out the negatives he inserted the top one in the enlarger and felt with his toe for the foot-action switch. Then, as he stood there in the subdued light of the little room, he heard the distant sound of the door buzzer.

For a second or two he stood immobile, muttering under his breath and undecided about what he should do. He remembered that the living room lights were on and he knew they were visible from the street. This suggested that if anyone wanted to see him, there would be a lot more buzzing before the caller gave up. Then, aware that there was no particular hurry about the job at hand and curious about the identity of his caller, he pulled the sheet from the easel, slid it into the proper drawer, and closed the drawer to keep out the light.

A tug at the bow loosened the apron and he tossed it on

the counter. He took the pile of negatives and tipped the base of the easel a little so he could slide them underneath. Then he opened the door, snapped off the safelight and went out, closing the door behind him. He had one more thought as the buzzer sounded again and, perhaps because the experience at Frank Kirby's place was still fresh in his mind, he took time to detour into the bedroom.

There was a .32 Colt automatic in the drawer of the bedside table. Although he had had it for many years—he did not think they made the model any more—it had been well cared for and it still looked like new as he lifted it and felt the oily coolness against his palm. Because he had not examined it in years, he checked the action and the clip before he jacked a shell into the chamber. Then, feeling just a little sheepish because such precautions were so foreign to him, but stubborn too when he remembered the negatives and the attempt that had been made the night before to locate them, he started for the door.

Apparently whoever was at the door was beginning to get annoyed because this time when the buzzer came to life the sound was continuous. Someone was leaning on it and the rasp of it jarred Murdock and he yelled ahead.

"All right!" he said, with mounting irritation. "All right!"

The buzzing stopped and so did Murdock as he glanced at the automatic and wondered what he was going to say if the caller turned out to be some friend of his. Where, he asked himself, was he going to put the damn gun?

And so, more embarrassed now than concerned, he saw his jacket and put it on. He shoved the automatic into the right-hand pocket and kept his hand on it as he reached out to turn the latch with his left. He twisted the knob and opened the door part way, still standing behind it. Then he let go of the gun, very glad that he had hidden it, as

Keith Howard hurried past him, his young face strangely grim.

"Have you seen Sally?" he demanded.

"Sally?"

"Sally Fisher."

Murdock shut the door and looked again at the young reporter, remembering the office gossip which had it that they were in love and expected to get married the next time Howard got a raise.

"No," he said. "Did you try her apartment?"

"Naturally I tried her apartment," Howard said, his voice jerky and high pitched with strain. "Four times I called there. I finally went over and practically forced the janitor to open up so I could be sure nothing had happened to her. She wasn't there."

He pulled out a pack of cigarettes, and when he tried to extract one his fingers trembled so violently he dropped it. When he finally got it in his mouth he forgot to light it and by now Murdock could see the wild look in his eyes as they roved the room, the fine film of perspiration on the worried face.

"She didn't come to work at all," he said.

Something about the cadence of his voice and the things he said were contagious. In spite of himself Murdock became aware of a mounting apprehension.

"I even tried the police," Howard said. "They couldn't tell me a thing—or wouldn't."

He was moving about the room now, not looking for anything but simply because he seemed unable to stand still. Not until he came to the mirror and caught sight of himself did he stop. He ran a finger inside the neckband of his shirt, which was damp like his face; he tried to straighten his bow tie.

"What made you think she might be here?" Murdock said.

"I couldn't think of any place else to go. And I know she likes you. She told me once if she ever had any trouble or some problems, if she didn't know what to do, she'd want to talk to you."

"Why not you? You're in love with her, aren't you?"

"What's that got to do with it?" Howard cried out in his uncertainty. "Some things you'd rather talk over with somebody else, even a stranger. And you're older and—oh, how the hell do I know? All I know is she's gone and—"

He stopped abruptly and picked something from the table beneath the mirror. Murdock could not see what it was, but he saw the youth stare at it and then he was striding forward, his face stiff and his eyes blazing. He opened his clenched fist under Murdock's nose and Murdock saw the lipstick and remembered how Sally had stood in front of the mirror that morning working with it.

"It's hers," Howard said savagely. "I'd recognize it anywhere."

"Okay," Murdock said. "Take it easy. She—"

Howard did not even hear him. "Don't lie to me!" He shouted. "Where is she? God damn you, Murdock—"

He swung his right then, a wild impulsive blow that was probably born of desperation and hysteria. With no chance to duck or even to understand what was happening, Murdock was clubbed on the side of the head; because he was a bit off balance he went down, smack on his haunches and more surprised than hurt.

He nearly got up, for it was instinct that prodded him and anger came quickly. Then, somehow, he saw the anguished look on Howard's face and understood that if he stood up he might have to swing in self-defense. Instead he reached back into the realm of reason and stayed put, his dark gaze intent and his voice curt and aggressive.

"She was here this morning," he said, wanting somehow to jar some sense into the young reporter's head. "She went from here to the police."

That one word did it. Howard's mouth opened and the unlighted cigarette dangled from his lower lip.

"The police? Why? What—"

Murdock cut him off. Remembering that Howard could not know what had happened to Sally Fisher the night before, he began to talk. In clipped, impatient tones he explained how she had been attacked. He tried to explain why as he told of the work she had done for Tom Brady.

"Lieutenant Bacon asked her to try to remember all she could," he said. "She went to see him this morning. She came here first to ask me if she should."

He stood up, still a little wary, and brushed off his trousers while Howard removed the cigarette from his mouth and a flush began to tint his cheeks. Without actually moving, Howard seemed to sag and then as though fully understanding what he had done, he said, his voice husky with shame and awe:

"I don't know what got into me. You should have clouted me. Jesus, I'm sorry."

"Forget it," Murdock said. "What you need is a drink."

"No. That's all right." He paused and once again his gaze grew cloudy. "But where is she now, Kent? The police wouldn't keep her all this time. Suppose—"

"It's no good supposing. If I were you I'd keep ringing her apartment. Or if it'll make you feel any better, go over there and wait. It's not very late yet and maybe the police haven't finished. When they do they'll see she gets home all right."

He hesitated, not yet admitting his own concern but not liking the advice he had given Howard.

"I'll tell you what," he said. "You go home and park by the telephone. Give me a chance to scout around and see what I can find out."

"But," protested Howard with commendable logic, "if she should know something important, she could be in danger."

"If the police think so they'll take no chances. You can bank on that. Let me talk to Lieutenant Bacon—he's handling the case. Maybe he'll talk to me when he wouldn't to you. . . . Go on now." He eased him over to the door and opened it. "Give me an hour. I'll call you at your place. You've got a telephone, haven't you? Well, write down the number for me."

He waited while Howard made the notation on a piece of copy paper he found in his pocket. He tore off a corner and gave it to Murdock.

"I guess you're right," he said. "But you'll call? For sure?"

Murdock said he would. He waited until the reporter started toward the stairs and then he closed the door and went over to the telephone. For a moment he thought about the negatives in the darkroom and then he knew they could wait. He took the automatic out of his pocket and put it in a drawer. He dialed a number, asked for Bacon's office, and was informed that the lieutenant was out.

"We expect him back," the voice said, "but you never know."

"Tell him I called," Murdock said. "If he comes in before I get there tell him I said to wait."

Lieutenant Bacon was sitting at his desk with his hat and coat on and one of his Little Wonder Panatelas in his mouth. He eyed Murdock aslant without moving his head and his greeting was gruff but not unfriendly.

"Now what?" he said. "And make it snappy. I want to get home."

"What did you do with Sally Fisher?"

"Why?"

"I'll tell you why," Murdock said. "When she stopped by my place this morning and I sent her over here she forgot her lipstick. Her boy friend, one of our reporters named Keith Howard, just came over and found the lipstick and suggested I'd kidnapped her. He knocked me on my can."

Bacon's eyes opened and things happened behind them.

"That's what you get for fooling around with other guys' girls," he said dryly. "Did he get away with it?"

"It's not funny," Murdock said. "The poor guy was half crazy. He's been looking for her all day; he made the janitor open her apartment. . . . She didn't come to work," he said accusingly.

"We cleared that with your office."

"Ahh," said Murdock. "Then she's all right."

"Certainly she's all right."

Murdock's breath came out in an audible sigh of relief. He realized now that he had been more alarmed than he was ready to admit, but he was not yet satisfied.

"You're not still holding her here, are you?"

"Nope."

"Where is she?"

"You can say she's a guest of the city. In a suite, with room service and everything."

"Alone?"

"With a policewoman."

Murdock thought it over and watched Bacon savor his cigar. He rolled it gently between his lips. He worked on it in tidy puffs and his unconcern was so studied and self-satisfied that Murdock found it irritating.

"Don't be so damn smug," he shouted. "If Sally's in some hotel here I can locate her in fifteen minutes."

"You're bragging," Bacon said, refusing to be nettled. "Maybe you could flush her in an hour. You find the hotel and the room, and you go up there and try to get in and you know what happens? I'll tell you. That little police-woman of mine will put the collar on you and don't think she won't."

He tipped his chair and his feet hit the floor as he sat up. "You think I'm kidding? You start nosing around and you'll find out. You'll get yourself pinched and if you do I'll hold you overnight, so help me. What the hell do you think this is, some parlor game?"

Murdock stuck his chin out. "All right," he said. "Now tell me you think Sally's going to give you a verbatim account of those reports if you just give her time."

"You're slipping, son," Bacon said. "You're losing your grip. You ain't thinking." He leaned forward. "The kid remembered a couple of things this morning and she thought she might remember more if she had time. We didn't want to hold her but we also remembered something maybe you've forgotten. If we know she typed Brady's reports, maybe somebody else knows it. Maybe by now the guy's worried about what she might remember. If the killer grabbed those reports it's because they're important to him. If the girl knows anything that can tag him—I don't say she does, but our guy can't be sure of that—she could get hurt."

"Okay," Murdock said, chagrined by his protests and impressed by the things Bacon had said. "Just forget I stopped in."

"I wish I could," Bacon said calmly. "We explained it

to her," he said. "The best we could without scaring her. We said we'd appreciate it if she would try to remember more details and that we'd take care of her job. We asked your boss to keep it quiet." He shrugged. "We didn't know about the boy friend, and she forgot to tell us."

He stood up and settled his hat the way he wanted it. "I'm going home if you haven't got anything more than this on your mind."

Murdock thought about the negatives and decided not to get into an argument about them now. It was not that he felt any need to withhold the information from Bacon so much as the desire to complete his printing and find out just exactly what he had before he committed himself.

"Okay to use your phone?" he asked.

"For what?"

"I told Howard I would call him."

"Go ahead," Bacon said. "Just be sure you don't tip our hand."

He waited while Murdock got an outside line and dialed his number. Then he was talking, his voice reassuring but uninformative.

"The police are taking care of her," he said. "No, not here. She's all right and they want to be sure she stays all right. So just act your age and simmer down. Why don't you take that drink I recommended."

"I will," Howard said. "I'll take it right now. And thanks, Kent. Thanks a million. I'm sorry I acted like such a jerk."

Murdock hung up and said that was that. Bacon said he was glad of it and together they left the office and went along the hall to the elevators.

16

WHEN Kent Murdock had locked himself in his apartment he went immediately to his darkroom and began to make prints of the negatives he had hidden under the easel. Such work was almost automatic to him now and because of the subject matter he did not have to worry about dodging the prints or giving them any particular attention. He had nine of these finished and hardening when, for the second time that night, he heard the imperative summons of the buzzer.

This time the sound angered him. Because of the things that had already happened since he went to the hospital to see Carey, his nerves were jumpy and his disposition much the worse for wear. Even so, his immediate reaction centered about his work and he took the proper precautions before he opened the door and stepped into the living room. Not until then did he make up his mind.

"To hell with it!" he said softly, glaring at the door. "Buzz, damn you! See if I care."

The sound came again, more insistent now, and he stayed where he was, bad tempered and obstinate.

He counted the third ring, and the fourth, and in his present mood he would have stayed there indefinitely if the pounding hadn't started. For this was not the discreet rapping of knuckles; the sound he now heard was more like the thump of a fist. He knew that if it continued it would arouse other tenants and so, boiling inwardly, he strode forward in self-defense, remembering the gun in the drawer and jamming it into his hip pocket before he turned the night latch.

He let go of the automatic the instant he opened the door. He stared, openmouthed in this first moment of wonderment and incredulity. He backed up as Rita Alderson lurched into the room and he smelled the strong odor of whisky before he noticed the glazed look in her eyes and the slackness of her face.

"What's the matter with you?" she said as she weaved past him. "You must be a sound sleeper." She wheeled unsteadily, spreading her legs for balance; then peered at him. "But no, you weren't even in bed. . . . You oughta get that buzzer fixed."

For a few seconds after he had closed the door Murdock just stared at her. She stood in the center of the room, weaving a bit as he approached, her smile lopsided and pathetic. She was wearing a brown gabardine skirt and a blue cashmere sweater and a camel's-hair coat that had nearly slipped from one shoulder.

Because he had never seen her like this it worried him. He had never known her to take more than two drinks and it had always seemed to him that she did this, not because of any appetite for liquor, but simply to be sociable and one of the party. He had seen drunken women before and a few had disgusted him. But he had no such feeling now as he studied the half-closed eyes and the slack red mouth which had been unevenly smeared with lipstick.

Even as he asked himself why this had happened she reached out and put her hands on his shoulders. With that the bag which had been under one arm thumped heavily to the floor, though he did not wonder about the sound at the time.

"Hey," he said, finding his voice at last. "What is this?"

"'Mmm a little drunk," she said. "Would've been drunker," she added, slurring her words, "if the place hadn't closed. Freddie's Bar," she said. "You know it? A real nice place."

He had to put his arms about her when she leaned on him. He had to hold her, feeling the rounded softness of her body beneath the sweater, heavy now that he had to support her weight. For a second or two she rested her forehead against his shoulder and then she tossed it back and tried to focus.

"You like me, don't you?"

"I think you're wonderful," Murdock said.

"Not wonderful," she said. "Just a little. Because of George. George was the one that thought you were wonderful and maybe I did too. Because I could talk to you and you treated me like a lady. . . . That's a laugh, isn't it?" she added as her voice trailed off. "Me a lady."

She drew her head back still further, peering up at him now. "But you don't have to worry. I don't want to sleep here, but you're my friend, aren't you?"

"Sure I'm your friend."

"Then all you got to do is give me a drink and some money, and I'll go quietly. 'S a promise."

Again her head fell forward and when she made no move Murdock slid a finger under the soft chin and tilted it back. Had it been a man he could have slapped his cheeks and given him a shake to make him pay attention. Now, when he tried to hold her away so she would look at him, she giggled.

"Look, Rita," he said. "This is no good."

"What's no good?"

"This. I mean—"

"You're my friend, aren't you?" she said without opening her eyes.

He did not answer this and in his mind there was only

confusion and, somehow, alarm. Because he had to know how such a thing could happen he wanted her attention. He reached for a lock of blonde hair that had fallen forward to obscure one eye, apparently for the lack of a bobby pin, and as he brushed it back he saw the bruise, not large, but bluish now at the side of her forehead.

He did not ask about it. He did not think it would do any good, but it suddenly came to him that this girl was afraid. Whatever had happened earlier had either frightened her or in some way so shattered her emotional balance that she could no longer cope with the situation by herself and she had turned to whisky as an antidote. He told himself it had to be that way. There could be no other explanation.

He withdrew his hand and tilted her chin again. "I'll tell you what I'll do."

"What?"

"I'll make the drink."

"Good."

"And then I'll take you home."

With that her eyes opened. "Oh, no." She tried to shake a finger at him, her smile suddenly crafty. "And let old Harriett see me like this? Wouldn't she like that?"

"She'll be in bed," Murdock said. "It's nearly two o'clock."

"Henderson won't be in bed," she said. "He'll know and he'll tell. . . . Nope," she said, in arbitrary tones. "Not little Rita. That's why I came here. 'Cause you're my friend."

"What about Jerry?"

"Go to Jerry with me like this? Are you kidding?"

She hiccuped and said: "Oops, excuse me," and then she was continuing her argument. "And besides Jerry wouldn't understand. I love the guy but he don't understand things

like you do. . . . Just give me ten dollars—spent all my
money buying Scotches and soda—and I'll go quietly."

"Where?"

"Why, to a hotel," she said, as if this was the most natural
thing in the world. "I'll buy me a bed."

That answered one of Murdock's unasked questions because now he knew what had been in her mind. Alone, and
not knowing whom to turn to, she had come to him, not the
girl he had known as his friend's wife, who, perhaps sensitive about her background, had always been conscious
that she must be a lady and use the manners and the lan-
guage expected of her. Because of Harriett—who had given
her permission for the marriage because of George's insist-
ence and a mother's fear of alienating him—Rita had always been on the defensive. Now she spoke with the usage
of one who had worked as a waitress and known the rough
edges of the entertainment world, not tough, but in the
vernacular and unconcerned about her tenses.

"A bed," she said. "That's all I need so I can shack up by
myself. Ten dollars, hunh? For a friend?"

"Okay," Murdock said, his mind beginning to fashion a
plan of his own.

For he was not sure Rita could even get to a hotel under
her own power. Even if she could she would attract attention that could be embarrassing. The other alternative, that
he take her to a hotel and help her register, had no appeal
at all and so, under the circumstances, she would have to
stay here.

He found a ten-dollar bill and gave it to her, watching
her peer at it closely before she thrust it into her coat
pocket. Then, to his surprise, she came up on tiptoe and
kissed the corner of his mouth with a soft, wet peck that
was no more than a gesture.

"You're a doll," she said.

"Sure," Murdock said. "You can tell me about it while we're having that nightcap."

"That's right. Gotta have one more for the road."

"Because you're scared?" Murdock said, softly and not sure she had heard him.

"How did you know?" she said, and then swayed sideways so that he had to hold her, first steadying her and then leading her to the divan.

When he went out to the kitchen she had her head back on the cushion and her eyes were closed. When he returned with the two drinks he thought she might have passed out, but when he spoke she opened her eyes. She sat up with an effort and took the glass.

"Cheers," she said, and took a swallow of whisky and water. She made a face and then, as though the devil were driving her, emptied the glass. When she looked at him her chin was wet and she leaned forward. "Just what I needed," she said and, her eyelids closing, let the glass slip from her fingers.

Murdock was on his feet as she sagged and he caught her before she could topple forward. He held her that way until he could fix a cushion and then he eased her body into the corner so that her head looked comfortable.

For a long moment he looked down at her, knowing somehow that this was the best way even as he felt the pressure of the growing disturbance in his mind. For that brief interval his dark gaze was soft with understanding and pity and then, remembering the unfinished business in his darkroom, he turned quickly away.

This time, because of some intuitive impulse he did not bother to analyze, he locked the door behind him. He made the five remaining prints. One by one he put the first batch on his small ferrotyper, squeezing out the excess water and waiting until they buckled before taking them off. When he made a pile of these and put the negatives on top, he repeated the process with the more recent prints. Then, taking time to clean up, he let himself out of the room and locked the door behind him.

The girl had not moved from the corner of the divan, and after he had carried his work to the bedroom he came back to look down at her. For a second or two he considered trying to rouse her. If it had been a man—or some women— he could have managed. A pot of coffee brewing while he removed the clothing, or most of it, and then a forcible submission under a cold shower had done the trick before. But his better judgment told him to let well enough alone.

Gently then, he raised her body sufficiently to free the camel's-hair coat, and only when he held it up did his thoughts turn back and hang on a known fact that jarred him strangely. He tried to dismiss this thought but it would not go and now he took another look at the coat, aware that in its present condition it did not measure up to Rita's careful standards. The quality of the material was excellent but the coat was wrinkled. It had been a long time since it had been pressed—or did it seem so because it had been wet?

Not tonight. There had been no rain. But what of the tall girl in such a coat who had come out of Brady's building and darted toward the corner in that brief downpour while Frank Kirby had watched from across the street?

Now, unable to think beyond the troublesome question, not even wanting to speculate, he folded the coat and put it on a near-by chair. In the bedroom closet he found a pillow and an extra blanket. He had already decided that chivalry and the desire for his guest's comfort could better be ignored, everything considered. For it was one thing to give his room to a sober woman and something else again to take the risk with someone in Rita's condition. Suppose, when she woke to find herself in bed, she forgot what had happened the night before?

"Unh-unh," he said softly. "Not tonight."

And so he did the best he could with what he had, lifting her limp form slightly so he could get her body flat, removing the spectator pumps and straightening the legs, putting the pillow under the blonde head and then tucking the blanket lightly about her before he stepped back.

Her handbag still lay on the rug and when he picked it up its weight surprised him. He carried it to the chair, intending to put it on her coat and then, prompted by some impulse he did not bother to classify, he opened it and saw the automatic pistol buried beneath the heterogeneous clutter of personal effects.

Absently then, he put the bag aside, his gaze narrowed and intent as he weighed the gun in one palm and identified it as a small calibre Mauser with plain wooden stocks, lighter than most American guns firing the same type bullet. Not thinking any more about it, he slipped out the clip and, tipping the gun sideways, jacked out the shell in the chamber so that it fell on the coat.

He thumbed more bullets out of the clip. Together with the one in the chamber there were six in all, and when he tested the spring he knew the clip would hold at least two more shells. He smelled the muzzle and could only guess that it had not been fired recently. The fact that the gun had not been loaded to capacity meant nothing in itself since not everyone made a habit of using a full clip; it saved the spring to carry a lesser number of shells unless a particular occasion demanded more.

But it bothered him nevertheless. It supported his hunch
that fear of some sort had brought Rita here when alcohol
proved insufficient to give her courage, and now, as he replaced the automatic, his glance strayed to the locked door
of his darkroom.

When he had turned out all the lights but the one
nearest the divan, he went through the short hall to his
bedroom, thinking now of the prints and the negatives that
luck had brought him after Tom Brady had worked so hard
to get them. Not until then did it occur to him that Rita's
drunkenness was anything but genuine and it shocked him
a little as the alternative came to him. She had been drinking. But she also had at one time been an actress and if
she—

He put the supposition from his mind, deciding he was
too tired and confused to do it justice. But he did take a
precaution. When he closed his door he turned the key,
his grin humorless and eyes brooding as he reminded himself that locking a woman *out* of his room was something
of a switch.

17

KENT MURDOCK did not immediately think of his uninvited guest when he opened his eyes the next morning.
He had overslept by fifteen minutes and it took him a while
to get his mind clicking and his memory working on the
things that had happened the night before. But when the
truth came to him he jumped out of bed and reached for
his robe, not caring whether this was the proper way to

confront a lady before breakfast but wanting to see what
had happened.

He gave a tug at the doorknob until he remembered he
had locked it before going to bed. He gave the key an
impatient twist and stepped into the little hall, craning his
neck as he leaned part way through the living room doorway. He saw at once that the divan was empty but he
still was not satisfied and called out.

"Rita?" Tentatively. "Rita?" More loudly this time.

By then he could see that the coat and bag were gone,
so he went barefoot into the living room and kitchen to
make sure he was alone. While there he put water on for
his coffee, not surprised that she was gone and a little
grateful when he thought how embarrassing it might have
been, for her at least, if he had found her still asleep. The
knowledge had a salutary effect on his frame of mind and
gave him a chance to look ahead with anticipation to the
prints he had made the night before but not yet examined.

By the time he had shaved and showered the water was
ready for his coffee, and while it dripped he dressed, resisting the impulse to take a peek at the photographs until
he had his orange juice. There was no bread left for toast
so he took his coffee back to the bedroom and then,
straightening out the bed as best he could, he spread the
prints out on top of it. Without making an effort to examine
them in any sort of order, he glanced at one after the other,
not exactly reading them but absorbing facts and details
until a rough pattern of understanding began to unfold in
his mind. There were ten minutes of this concentrated
effort before he heard the buzzer, and this time he swore
softly, not angrily but with resignation.

How, he asked himself, could he avoid this incessant
interruption? What did he have to do, move? The place

was getting to be like South Station and for a moment as he stood up he glared in the general direction of the hall door. Then, as the humor of the situation began to undermine his irritation, he gathered up the prints, stacked them, and looked about for some place to put them.

Impulsively then, he lifted the mattress and slid them in on top of the box spring. The negatives he tucked into the inside pocket of a gray flannel suit hanging in the closet. Sliding a gray jacket from its hanger he started for the door as the buzzer ended its second summons, and by this time he was no longer annoyed. For in his present frame of mind, buoyed up as it was with the knowledge he had so recently gained, he did not particularly care who wanted to see him and it did not surprise him much when he opened the door to find Jerry Alderson standing there.

Alderson's entrance was tentative and uncertain. His brown eyes looked worried and his brow was furrowed and there was a certain apologetic hesitancy to his speech.

"I was hoping I'd catch you," he said as he entered. "I— it's about Rita. Do you know where she is?"

"No," said Murdock, glad that he could speak the truth.

"I thought she might have called."

"Oh? Why would she do that?"

"She didn't come home last night," Alderson said, and it was now apparent that the uncertainty in his glance was based on worry. "Henderson says she went out some time after ten. She didn't come back."

"You didn't see her last night?"

"No."

He started to move about the room, eyes probing before him, and the way he acted reminded Murdock of Keith Howard. For although Jerry was older and chunkier and clad in better fitting and more expensive clothes, he had the same air of suspicion about him. Now when his gaze fastened on the divan Murdock said:

"What made you think she'd come here?"

"I didn't think so. I just had to be sure. She hasn't many friends and—"

"How about Denham?"

"He wasn't in."

The reply came absently and there was a sudden change in attitude as Alderson stopped, nostrils dilating as he began to sniff. Unconsciously Murdock imitated him and it was not until then that he became aware of the faint but unmistakable fragrance that hung over the room. He had not noticed it last night, perhaps because the smell of liquor was so strong, but it was here now and it was definitely not a male odor.

Now he watched Alderson lean over the divan, his misgivings rising. He saw the other lift the pillow and sniff again. The blanket which had been twisted aside was lifted and then Alderson pounced on something wedged in the cushions. When he wheeled and held up the handkerchief, Murdock knew he was in for trouble.

He shifted his weight as Alderson strode toward him, remembering what Howard had done and quickly deciding that once was enough. He did not know whether talk would help but he spoke quickly as Alderson stopped and his hands clenched. The gleam in the bright brown eyes was the tip-off and Murdock said:

"Don't swing unless you're ready to duck. . . . Sure she was here," he said, his tone curt, impatient, and hard. "Why? Because she was afraid. Afraid to go home. Afraid to come to you. She had a bruise on her face where somebody clipped her." He took a breath and in a last effort to shock some sense into the man said: "She was drunk."

That did it. Alderson blinked and something happened deep in his eyes. He swallowed and a different sort of anger came.

"That's a lie," he said in outraged tones.

"Who hit her?" Murdock demanded, still on the offensive. "You?"

"God, no!" Alderson's face twisted, an almost horrified expression. "Me? I couldn't. I'm in love with her."

"Denham?"

"Denham? . . . Denham," he said with sudden savagery. "I'll kill him."

"Cut it out!" Murdock said brusquely. "Take it easy. I didn't say Denham hit her."

"But you said—what did she—"

"I'll tell you if you'll sit down and start using your head. Cool off! I want to talk to you. . . . How about a cup of coffee?"

Alderson sat down, his body limp and his belligerence vitiated by the things he had heard. His good-looking face was shiny with perspiration now and he took the handkerchief from his breast pocket to wipe it off.

"Yeah," he said. "I could use a cup if it isn't too much trouble. . . . Black."

When Murdock brought the coffee Alderson had slumped in the chair and his eyes held a distant look. He thanked Murdock as he accepted the cup.

"Why should she come to you?" he asked quietly.

Murdock said he did not know. Without going into details he explained how Rita had fallen asleep and spoke of her determination not to go home. He said it seemed best to let her sleep there on the divan.

"She was gone when I woke up," he said.

"You don't know where."

"No. But when she gets over her hangover she'll probably go home. . . . How much would you stand to lose,"
he said in swift digression, "if your mother decided to cut
you out of her will?"

Alderson, in the act of taking a sip of coffee, stopped,
the cup in mid-air.

"What?"

"How big is your mother's estate?"

"I don't know," Alderson said. "A lot of it's tied up in the
company. She's not rich by today's standards. Maybe she
has an income of forty or fifty thousand a year."

"If you capitalized that conservatively that would be
maybe a million and a half, not counting the house or any
insurance she might have."

"Wait a minute." Alderson put aside the cup. "What the
hell is this?"

"I'm looking for motives for murder," Murdock said
flatly. "You've got one."

"Me? You think I—"

Murdock cut him off. "Your father left most of his estate
in trust for you and your brothers, didn't he? With George
gone you and Donald will split it."

"What about it?"

"There was a funny clause in the will, giving your
mother power to cut either of you off if you married without her consent. What I'm wondering is—does she know
you married somebody named Elsie Graham in San Francisco in 1951 and that a divorce was granted in Reno about
eight weeks later."

Alderson's face was suddenly white and stiff at the
mouth and his brown gaze was contemptuous.

"You're a proper bastard, aren't you?"

"Your mother hired Tom Brady," Murdock said, ignoring the comment. "She wanted to know a lot of things about a lot of people. What Brady turned up about you was probably nothing but routine to him, but that's the way he worked. I don't think he went to California to check on you but while he was out there he did a job."

"That was a long time ago."

"Granted. My point is simply that Brady didn't live to turn in his reports. If he was killed because of them it could follow that he was killed by someone who was afraid to let your mother read those reports; someone who had plenty to lose. It could be you."

Alderson had his temper in hand now. He stood up and scoffed at the assumption. "You're nuts," he said. "Maybe I was scared at the time, but not any more. She wouldn't crack down on me for that now. If I explained it to her she'd understand."

He lit a cigarette and began to pace back and forth, the cadence of his voice remote, as though he were talking to himself.

"I had a thirty-day leave before I shoved off for Korea," he said. "Like a lot of guys at the time I wasn't sure I'd be back so another fellow from my company and I decided to live it up. We had a glow on most of the time and this fellow had a girl. She had a friend for me and we did the town for a few days until this guy got the idea he wanted to get married. The four of us went to get the marriage license and I was just tanked enough to apply for one too. Anyway, we flew to Las Vegas because we couldn't wait. We got married, all of us."

He stopped pacing long enough to stab out his cigarette and said: "We stayed there four or five days and by the time I got back to San Francisco and sobered up I knew what I had—a part-time hooker and a full-time lush. . . .

A tramp," he said, "and nobody to blame but myself. That's when I got scared that mother might hear about it. I was scared silly. It was like a nightmare and when I realized I never could be sure what Elsie might do after I'd gone, I went to a lawyer.

"I had about eight thousand bucks left from what I got when Dad died and I put it on the line. I'd pay for six weeks in Reno. When Elsie delivered the divorce to the lawyer she was to get what was left. That looked like a lot of money to her and she took it. The divorce came through and I've never seen her since."

The intensity of the explanation was convincing and the facts as Alderson told them were understandable. Murdock believed him but in his own mind nothing changed. Because Alderson now asserted that the truth could do him no harm did not make it so. He started to say so but the other had not finished.

"How come you know so damn much about those reports?" he said coldly. "I thought they were stolen."

"They were," Murdock said. "But I took some pictures of certain things that Brady picked up. He had a copy of your marriage application and an affidavit on the divorce."

"Okay," Alderson said, disgustedly. "You can't sell them to me so go ahead and try my mother if you like."

Murdock took it. So long as he continued to pry into the affairs of others he had to expect a certain amount of abuse and contempt. He colored slightly as he rose but his voice was level and controlled.

"All I'm interested in is Tom Brady," he said.

"Then I'll tell you something else." Alderson hesitated, as though he wanted to accent his words. "I didn't kill him and neither did Barry Denham."

"Oh?"

"I was hanging around the Clay looking for Denham."

"This was after you had dinner with your client?"

"Yes, and if Brady was murdered around nine or a little after, Denham didn't do it. I saw him come out of the hotel a couple of minutes after nine. I followed him to the Club Saville and he was still there when I left."

"That alibi for Denham works two ways."

"What?"

"It's an alibi for you."

Alderson thought it over; finally he shrugged. "All I'm saying—"

Whatever he had in mind was left unsaid because the shrill ring of the telephone cut him off. When Murdock answered it the familiar voice of Lieutenant Bacon came to him, blunt and businesslike.

"I'm giving you a break, son," he said. "This one didn't go out over the air so if you get on your horse you might beat the rest of the press boys." He mentioned an address and said: "Denham."

"What?"

After that Murdock listened as Bacon rattled off the essential facts and hung up.

He replaced the telephone and looked at Alderson.

"There goes your alibi," he said.

Alderson frowned uncertainly. "How do you mean?"

"They just found Denham in his car with a slug in his head. They think it happened sometime before midnight."

He went over to pick up his camera and equipment case. "I'm going down there now. Want to come?"

Alderson seemed to have difficulty grasping the significance of what he had heard. The frown dug deeper across his brow and he swallowed visibly. Murdock was almost to the door before he seemed to shake himself and find his voice.

"Me?" he said with a rising inflection. "Good God, no!"

He hurried forward and waited for Murdock to open the door. As he went out he mumbled something about being late for an appointment at his office.

18

THE STREET was a narrow, one-way affair which branched off Kneeland and was lined on both sides with small loft buildings and wholesale houses. A policeman had been stationed at the intersection to divert traffic and as Murdock made the turn he was flagged down until he identified himself and said Bacon had asked him to come.

"Okay," the man said, "but you'd better park here and walk down. It's going to be jammed up a bit."

Murdock edged into the curb and took out his camera and case. He could see the ambulance in the middle of the street as he approached and then, beyond the two police cars at the curb, he saw the huddle about a sedan parked just ahead. When he reached the edge of the gathering he saw the three men struggling to remove a body from the front seat of the sedan, and now he put the case down and checked his camera.

He got a passable shot as a stretcher was loaded into the rear of the ambulance, and when the flashbulb went off in the shadowy canyon it attracted attention. Bacon stepped forth from the huddle about the sedan, his expression suggesting he was about to give forth with certain reprimands until he saw who had taken the picture.

"All right," he said. "You got one. That's enough. The other boys'll be accusing me of favoritism as it is."

The doors of the sedan stood open and as Murdock moved closer he saw that the glass had been broken in one of the windows. When he remembered that Bacon had said death had occurred sometime before midnight he wondered why the body had gone so long undiscovered. The answer that came to him was based on the broken glass and on the character of the street itself, which, although devoted to commerce by day, would be normally darkened and deserted at night. Bacon verified the hunch.

"The beatman finally got curious," he said. "Noticed the car earlier but didn't bother to take a close look. . . . He was on the floor," he said.

"Who?"

"Denham, who do you think? Sort of wedged between the front seat and the dash. Just walking by you couldn't see him. The car looked empty and the doors were locked from the inside, keys in the switch. That's why we had to break the glass."

"Could it be suicide?"

"It's possible. He was shot behind the right ear but I guess he could do it without breaking his arm. One shot. The gun on the seat beside him. . . . But I doubt if the body got down there on the floor like that by itself. Looks more like somebody pushed it there because he didn't want anybody nosing around. The longer it went undiscovered the harder to establish the time of death."

"Before midnight?" Murdock said.

"The M.E. thinks between eleven and twelve, but he's not going out on any limb." His glance slid past Murdock and he scowled. "Nuts," he said, speaking to no one. "Here they come."

Murdock looked round and identified the advancing phalanx as assorted members of the Press. Bacon tugged on his arm.

"You got a car?"

"Yes."

"All right. I'm about finished here and I've got to shake your pals. Meet me in front of the Clay in fifteen minutes. I want to talk to you."

By then the circle of reporters and photographers had started to form and Bacon was going into his speech. Murdock spotted the two *Courier* representatives and motioned them aside. He slipped the photographer his film holder and asked him to take it in. He spoke quietly to the reporter even as Bacon addressed the others.

"I'll give you what I've got," he said. "Anything else you'll have to get later. . . . A guy named Barry Denham. Had a room at the Clay Hotel. Shot once in the head. The gun on the seat beside him and the body on the floor. . . ."

Murdock moved off, hearing Bacon conclude his statement and refuse to answer additional questions. The cop at the corner let him back his car so he would not have to go down the street and then he headed for the Clay.

Lieutenant Bacon and his crew took over most of Denham's hotel room so that in the beginning Murdock made himself small and sat over in one corner to watch and listen and think. By that time he knew that a box of shells had been found here in a suitcase and that the calibre matched the gun which had been found on the seat of the sedan.

The assumption made was that Denham had been shot

with his own gun, just as Tom Brady had been killed with his gun, and what Murdock could not forget was the automatic he had found in Rita Alderson's bag. That gun had apparently not been fired recently but in the proper hands it would have served to disarm a man, even a man like Denham. The actual mechanics of the murder did not seem important at the moment and Murdock did not waste time thinking about it, and presently the men Bacon had assigned to investigate Denham's movements the night before began to report.

The first detective came in and read from some notes he had made. "Denham had a caller around six thirty," he said, and then his glance picked out Murdock and fixed there. "One of the bellboys recognized him."

"Who was it?" Bacon said.

"Murdock."

Bacon eyed Murdock aslant. "That's what you get for being so well known," he said dryly. "How long were you here?"

Murdock told him and then, seeing the glass on the bureau which Denham had used for his drink, he said: "You might get some prints from that glass."

"We already got prints," Bacon said. "From the corpse. . . . You can tell me what you talked about in a few minutes," he said, and gave his attention to the detective. "What else?"

"Denham came back here about ten fifteen."

"Okay."

"There were two phone calls after that. Denham made the first one," the detective said and gave the number.

"Did you check it?"

"Edward Alderson's residence, on Beacon."

"Ahh," said Bacon and when he looked at Murdock

again his gray gaze had narrowed. "What time was that?"

"According to the operator's record, at ten twenty-one. . . . The second call came at eleven fifteen, from outside. That's all I've been able to get on that one."

"Any other callers?"

"One. A woman."

"Anybody know her?"

"No, but she's been to see Denham before."

"What'd she look like?"

"Fairly tall, blonde, wore a camel's-hair coat."

Bacon looked at Murdock again but he did not make a production out of it. He rocked on heel and toe and nodded, his thin face somber.

"Put a scarf and dark glasses on her and she could pass for the one who came to see Brady the other night. . . . What time did she come?"

"Before eleven."

"How long before eleven? Ten minutes? A half hour?"

"A few minutes. That's as close as I could get it."

"When did she leave?"

"Probably before eleven thirty."

"What do you mean, probably?"

"Nobody saw her leave," the detective said, "but I found a guy who saw Denham go out at twenty after eleven."

"Alone?"

"Yeah. Took the side door and was seen heading for the parking lot across the street."

While Bacon was digesting the information, Sergeant Keogh, who had been searching the closet, demanded his attention.

"Here's something," he said. "The suitcase had a slit in the lining. These were tucked inside."

From where he sat, Murdock could not be sure what

Keogh had found but to him they looked like cards, or small pieces of paper. He watched Bacon examine them, heard him say: "Good enough." Then, still holding the new evidence in his hand, Bacon walked toward him.

"What did you talk about last night?" he asked. "How come you stopped in to see Denham?"

Murdock thought a moment and found the question difficult to answer. Beyond the hope that he could pick up some usable information he had no clear-cut reason why he had wanted to see Denham.

"I was trying to find out what I could about his background," he said finally. "About the California part. I asked if he knew anyone named Benjamin Danton out there."

"Why?"

"What?"

"Where'd you get that name from?"

Murdock hesitated again, thinking first of the prints he had hidden under the mattress, knowing that he would tell Bacon about them but not wanting to do it here.

"I remembered seeing it when I photographed those papers for Brady."

"In what connection?"

Murdock scowled, his eyes puzzled because he was unable to sense the direction of Bacon's thoughts. He said so.

"You saw the name," Bacon said with admirable patience. "So what was it on? A license, an affidavit—"

"Oh," Murdock said. "It was on three things. That's how I remembered it. A birth certificate," he said, "a marriage license, a transcript of a police record."

"Your hunch wasn't too bad," Bacon said, and held out the three cards in his hand. "Denham knew Benjamin Danton, all right."

When Murdock leaned forward, the name seemed to

jump at him and he saw all three—a California driver's license, a social security card, and an A.F.L. union card—had been made out to Benjamin Danton.

"Two sets of cards," Bacon said. "For a guy like him it wouldn't be too hard to get the ones he showed us the other night. . . . Barry Denham," he said, as though the words made an unpleasant taste in his mouth. "I'll bet he was no more an actor than you are. The hell of it is I was just beginning to line him up for the Brady thing."

Murdock stood up. He said if Bacon no longer needed him he'd be on his way.

"Go ahead," Bacon said. "Me, I'm going to pay a short call on the Aldersons. The D.A.'ll be in this for sure now and they might as well know it."

Murdock had the same thing in mind but now he knew he would have to wait, and so he went downstairs, turning toward the side entrance. He had parked his car in the lot that Denham had used, but as he stood there another thought came to him. After a glance down the street, he walked to the corner and looked both ways. When, half-way down the block, he saw a sign that said: Freddie's Bar, he started toward it.

The clock at the far end of the room said it was twenty minutes after twelve when Murdock walked into the dimly lighted interior. It was a small place, quiet now, with a long bar on the left and a dozen or so tables on the right topped with black glass. There were only three customers at the bar and Murdock kept his distance as he ordered a beer. When it came he asked the barman if he worked nights.

"Not this week."

"When do you go off?"

"Six."

Murdock said he was from the *Courier*. He said he would like to talk to the man who had been on duty the night before and could the barman give him his name and telephone number.

"Sure." The fellow consulted a small notebook next to the cash register. "Sam Marcus," he said, and read off the telephone number. "He'll be here at six but if you want him before that you can give him a ring."

Murdock thanked him. He finished his beer and stepped into the telephone booth to dial the number. A pleasant-voiced woman answered. When she said Mr. Marcus was out and asked if she could take a message, Murdock said he would call again.

19

WHEN Kent Murdock went back to his office after lunch Delaney, who was still filling in for him, said that a woman had called twice but would not give her name.

"Said she'd call again," he said. "Here, sit down."

"Stay there," Murdock said, "you're handling the job."

"Then how about you handling it for ten minutes while I duck across the street for a quickie?"

Murdock laughed and said all right. He sat down behind his desk, checked the assignment book, and glanced automatically at the monitor which told him which of the company cars were in use. He had a cigarette burning and was staring out the window when the telephone rang. The voice was instantly familiar.

"Kent?" Rita Alderson said. "I've been trying to get you."

"How do you feel?"

"Not good. Not good, but better. I think I'll live. I'm terribly ashamed about last night. I've never done a thing like that before and—"

Murdock interrupted her because he could tell she was embarrassed and finding the going difficult. He said it was nothing to be ashamed of.

"What time did you leave?"

"About eight o'clock. At first I didn't know where I was. I had this frightful head and I couldn't remember how I got there. Then I did remember and I found the ten dollars in my pocket, and I couldn't go home then, not the way I looked and felt, so I came here and went to bed."

"Where?" Murdock said.

When there was no immediate answer he let the silence continue for a second or two before he said:

"Jerry was around this morning. He wanted to know if I knew where you were. He found a handkerchief of yours on the divan. He was sort of upset."

Again the silence.

"I'm sorry," she said finally. "But I'm glad I got out in time. I'm not ready to talk to him yet. I don't want to talk to anybody until I've had time to think."

"You can't just keep staying there, can you?"

"Not without more money," she said. "I didn't have any bags so I had to pay for the room in advance. I can't sign for anything and I had to eat something. If I tell you where I am do you have to tell anyone else?"

"Not right now anyway."

"And will you come and talk to me and bring me a little more money? . . . I'm at the Harvey House," she said, mentioning an old residential hotel outside the downtown district.

Murdock thought about Denham and wondered how long it would be before Rita saw an afternoon paper. He decided against telling her about the murder now, but there was something else he could do, something he had been thinking about all morning. When he understood that now was the time to do it he said:

"I'll be over a little later in the afternoon. How much money will you need?"

"Oh, just a few dollars. In case I want to stay here another night."

Murdock did not question the last statement. In his own mind he had an idea that Lieutenant Bacon would find her before then, once he discovered that she was missing, but all he said was that he would bring some cash with him.

Henderson, the Alderson butler, listened to Murdock's request with a hesitant sort of disapproval all his own.

"I'm not sure Mrs. Alderson will want to see you, Mr. Murdock," he said. "The police have been here and I know she's very upset."

"Will you ask her, Henderson?" Murdock said, as he stood half in and half out of the doorway. "Just tell her," he added, trying out a bluff, "that if she doesn't see me the police will probably be back in a very few minutes."

Henderson did not like the proposal but neither was he willing to take the responsibility of an outright refusal. "Come in, please," he said with obvious reluctance. "I'll give her your message."

He turned and went up the stairs, bald head gleaming and his thick torso bent at the waist. He moved soundlessly, and he returned the same way, saying nothing at all until he stood directly in front of Murdock.

"You'll find her in the drawing room," he said. "She asked me to tell you that she hopes you won't be long."

Harriett Alderson was sitting in her favorite wing chair, her back angling toward the river windows so that her thin patrician face was partly in shadow. She sat motionless as Murdock approached, her gaze fixed and imperious. She did not ask why he had come or invite him to sit down but spoke with cold directness.

"Henderson tells me that you gave me the choice of seeing you or the police."

"I had to tell him something," Murdock said.

"And you've been reduced to threats, is that it?"

"I think it's important."

"To whom? Is your interest due to any consideration for me, or my family? . . . I don't understand you, Kent. You were always welcome in this house—"

"Because of George."

"There were many others who came because they were friends of my children. Some I approved of and some I did not, but all were, I hope, treated with politeness and consideration. Well, there's a limit to everything. I don't know what you want but you might as well know that I do not intend to be badgered by you. The death of Mr. Brady was a tragic thing and I am deeply sorry because I liked him. The police seem to think that there may be a connection between his death and someone in the family. I happen to disagree but I recognize their authority in such matters. I do not recognize yours. Now what do you want?"

Murdock shifted his weight and felt the warmth in his face because he recognized the truth of what had been said. He *had* been welcome in this house and there had been the unstated impression that Harriett Alderson had liked him in her way. He liked no part of what he was about to do but, remembering Tom Brady, he knew that he had waited long enough.

"What did the police want?"

"They asked questions. Of me and Gloria. By now I suspect they are questioning Donald and Jerry. And all about this half brother of Rita's who came once for dinner and was never asked again. . . . As if we could possibly know who killed him," she added disdainfully. "They even asked to make a tour of the house."

"You mean they searched it?"

"How do you mean, search? . . . They asked about Rita and I said she wasn't here and hadn't come home at all last night. They seemed to think I was lying. That lieutenant, whatever his name is, insinuated that she was hiding here. I had Henderson take them through the house."

"But they didn't actually search it," Murdock said quickly. "You know, go through the desks and chests and—"

"Certainly not."

The answer gave Murdock new hope. "I'd like to," he said.

"What?"

"I'd like your permission to search Rita's rooms."

She leaned forward slightly in her astonishment before her mouth tightened.

"You certainly may not have my permission."

"It'll be easier that way."

"For me or for you?"

"For both of us. You don't want me here and I don't like being here under these circumstances. But I'm willing to bargain with you."

"There will be no bargain."

"If I find what I'm looking for," Murdock said, as though he had not heard, "I'll turn it over to you."

"No."

"All right." Murdock sighed and gestured emptily. "That's why I have to use threats. It's the only way I can get anywhere with you. . . . It's like this," he said. "I found out some things this morning. In some ways I know more than the police do because of the photographs I took for Tom Brady. I expect to tell Lieutenant Bacon what I know because in the end this has to be a police job. But I'd like to wait a little while. I'd like to talk to you first—if I find what I'm looking for."

He hesitated and said: "But if you don't want it that way then I'll have to tell the lieutenant now. When I do I'll guarantee he'll come back here with a search warrant. As a matter of fact I think he'll be back with one anyway. It's just a question of time once he finds Rita."

When Murdock spoke like that he was convincing and even Harriett seemed to realize that this was no empty threat. As though recognizing the statements for what they were, she said, nothing changing in her face or in the clipped, cold cadence of her voice:

"You know where to go. I'll be here when you finish."

Murdock got out as quickly as he could and climbed to the fourth-floor suite, making no sound as he moved upward and not knowing whether Gloria was still in the house or not. The small sitting room, which was done in pale-gray and ivory, presented no problem since it offered very little space for concealment. There was the chaise and a matching chair, odd tables and lamps, a small television set, and an antique maple table-desk and chair. When the three drawers revealed nothing of interest he went on into the bedroom.

The bureau, the lowboy, and the vanity yielded nothing to interest him and a glance into the bathroom was enough to stop him in the doorway. That left a dressing room and a huge closet, and when Murdock saw the three pieces of matched luggage stacked in one corner he reached for the largest case. Even as he picked it up he knew it was not empty. Something slid back and forth with a thump as he tipped it from side to side and now he put it flat on the floor and examined the fastenings. The manipulation of the keys he had in his pocket plus a bit of force sprung the lock and then he was looking at a bulging briefcase with Tom Brady's initials stamped on one side.

His discovery did not surprise him greatly and he sat there on the floor to examine the papers which had been crammed inside. Most of these were carbons of the reports Brady had accumulated in his brief career as a private investigator and it did not take Murdock long to find what he was looking for: two sets of sheets, an original and a carbon, held together with paper clips.

In a matter of minutes he had scanned the twenty-odd sheets in Brady's report. This served to supplement the documents he had collected and added very little to the assumptions Murdock had already made. When he was sure, he put the other reports back into the briefcase, replaced it, and put the suitcase back where he had found it.

Harriett Alderson was still in the wing chair, her cane propped against it and her hands in her lap. Her chin maintained its tilt of defiance, but for the first time her dark eyes seemed apprehensive as she saw Murdock approach and noticed the papers in his hands. When he had moved another chair so that he could be closer to her, he sat down.

"Brady was pretty pleased with the job he did for you," he said, "at least in the sense that he had accomplished

what he set out to do. He said that if he produced there
would be a nice bonus for him."

"That's true."

"How much?"

"I told him if I was satisfied with his work I would give
him twenty-five hundred dollars."

"He didn't leave much of an estate," Murdock said. "He
has a daughter and two grandchildren. I think he earned
the bonus and I'd like to be sure his daughter collects." He
offered the two reports. "This is what you bought," he said.
"They're yours now. Go ahead, read them."

He had to put the reports in her lap before she accepted
them and then she picked up her glasses from the chair-
side table. When she began to read Murdock lit a cigarette, not thinking about murder in the minutes that
followed but unable to forget the trouble this woman had
caused.

When, finally, she put the papers in her lap and glanced
up, her eyes looked frightened and now he put out his cigarette and spoke of the letter Brady had written to his
daughter.

"Brady made a point in that letter," he said. "He was
pleased with his success because he was a conscientious
man, but he did not like what he had done. He said if he
could afford it he would have preferred to repay you his
salary and expenses and destroy his report. Do you know
why?"

He paused and when she made no reply he said: "He
could see how much trouble his report might make. He
said maybe it was all right for you to play God with other
people's lives but for himself he wished he had never taken
the job. . . . Why," he said, "couldn't you let well enough

alone? Isn't a mother supposed to trust her sons? Aren't
they entitled to make their own mistakes?"

"You don't understand."

"No," Murdock said, "I don't. Was it jealousy? Because
you didn't approve of their wives? Or just because you
wanted to run their lives the way you managed your husband? You've dominated Donald so there's nothing left between him and Gloria; there never will be until he moves
out of here. You drove Jerry out—"

"What I did was for their own good."

"That's only your opinion. Where did you get the idea of
a private detective? What started it?"

"George," she said, her voice suddenly quiet. "What happened to George."

"It was an accident," Murdock said.

"I know that. My mind tells me that but I can't help
what I feel. Rita killed him, accident or not. . . . You
don't know what it's like to sit here day after day with
nothing to think about except the past. I had a lovely body.
I was proud of it and the things I could do. I was popular
and pretty and—"

"You still are," Murdock said.

"—all because a fool horse refused a jump I'm sentenced
to the life of a cripple. When I go out I have to have help.
The doctors have told me how long I can expect to live but
that does not worry me now. I admit I never felt Rita was
good enough for George but I accepted her. Because she
was George's wife I offered her a home. But when that man
came—I never did believe he was her half brother—I made
up my mind I was going to find out the truth about him
while I could. . . . And I didn't approve of the way Gloria
kept taking these trips by herself and leaving Donald. It
was just by accident that I found out she and Arthur

Enders were in Miami Beach at the same time, but I decided I had better know more about that too."

She said other things but Murdock no longer tried to follow her. For he had begun to understand some of the things that had made this woman what she was.

An accident had robbed her of the thing she had once prized the most—her physical loveliness. An accident had robbed her of her favorite son. And so she had sat here brooding about the injustices of life, suspicious, resisting change, wanting desperately to cling to what she had. What made the situation all the more ironic was that she had been right in her suspicions. She had proved what she wanted to prove but in doing so she had supplied the potentials for murder. Murdock could not forget that, even as some new sympathy for her plight began to build inside him.

"You proved your point," he said. "And you were right, if that's any satisfaction to you. You can send Brady's check to his lawyer," he said. "I'll give you his name and address when you want it."

"Get out."

She straightened her shoulders and to Murdock it seemed that her eyes were blinking back unwanted tears, though he could not tell whether they came from anger or from shame. For even now she remained indomitable, refusing to admit her mistakes.

"Unless you'd rather I called Henderson. I've had all the insolence I can stand for one day."

Murdock stood up. He said he knew the way out. He said that at the risk of appearing even more insolent he'd make a final suggestion.

"If I were you," he said, "I'd start practicing a little contriteness. Because if you don't—now that those closest to

you know what you've done to them—I have an idea you
and Henderson will wind up having this house to your-
selves."

He hesitated to see if she wished to say anything more.
When she stared back at him he turned and left the room,
fairly certain now that he knew who had killed Brady but
knowing also that the evidence at hand might be insufficient to convince a jury.

20

KENT MURDOCK did a lot of thinking on his way home
from the Alderson house on Beacon Street. He not only
considered the reports again but he thought about Lieutenant Bacon and in this respect his conscience bothered
him not at all. Technically, he was withholding information from the police, but he also knew that, in themselves,
the reports were no longer important.

Harriett Alderson had ordered them, she was going to
pay for them, and they concerned her family. So long as
he had the photographs of Brady's accumulated documents what Harriett did with the reports could remain her
business. The important fact was the certainty that Rita
had taken them from Brady's files after he was dead.

"So now what?" he asked himself.

The answers to this were many and varied and when,
finally, the germ of an idea began to take root in his brain
he knew that he would need a little assistance but, at least
in the beginning, not of the official variety. The name that
came to mind was Frank Kirby, and Murdock dialed the

office number as soon as he let himself into the apartment.

The reply he got came from the phone-answering service and informed him that Kirby was out but expected back within a half hour. Murdock left his name and number and then went into the bedroom to get the prints from between the mattress and springs. He was still considering them when Kirby called back.

"I've got a lead, Frank," Murdock said. "How busy are you going to be this afternoon?"

"Not very," Kirby said. "I've got a payroll delivery but I should be free by four. . . . Say, how about that guy Denham? I read in the paper that he got his."

"I'll tell you what I know when I see you. Do you want to stop by my office or shall I pick you up at yours?"

"Why don't you come by here," Kirby said. "I'll be waiting out front at four. . . ."

It was a quarter after three when Murdock reached the *Courier* and by then he knew what he wanted to do. He had brought the prints with him—rolled up and held in place with an elastic—and he felt it was time to show Lieutenant Bacon what he had. What happened then would depend on Bacon's reaction, his mood, and Murdock's ability to sell an idea that would certainly be resisted.

In preparation for the encounter, he telephoned police headquarters to make sure Bacon would be in his office, and then he went upstairs to the city room and asked to borrow a piece of equipment that was occasionally used on special assignments—a midget tape-recorder that weighed about three pounds and was no larger than the extended palm of his hand. This came equipped with a small but highly sensitive microphone and a cartridge with sufficient tape to record for an hour, and when he had it set the way he wanted it he put it in his equipment case, strapping the top of this loosely so he could slide his hand inside and set the machine in motion without opening the case.

Lieutenant Bacon was shuffling papers on his desk when Murdock entered his office at three thirty. His greeting was no more than a grunt, his attitude suggesting that he was a very busy man who would tolerate no nonsense. He asked what Murdock wanted and Murdock countered with a question of his own.

"Are you still holding Sally Fisher as a guest of the city?"

"Yep," Bacon said. "She's livin' in luxury. At least for today. With her, we're playing it safe."

"Did she remember anything she typed?"

"Quite a few things."

Bacon began to reshuffle his papers, his manner suggesting that there was nothing more to be said on the subject.

"Did any of it help?" Murdock said, persisting.

"Sure it helped."

Murdock waited for five seconds. When there was no amplification he changed the subject.

"What did you find out about Denham—or Danton?"

"Plenty," Bacon said. "We got a quick make from Washington. He's been in trouble before," he said. "Got a record in Los Angeles and a bad discharge from the Army. Nothing to show he ever was an actor. That Alderson dame—the blonde one—"

"Rita."

"—must've known all that."

"She knows a lot more," Murdock said. "That's why I came here. I'd like to make a little deal with you."

"No deal," Bacon said. "Not even a little one."

"Okay."

Murdock stood up. He had no intention of leaving but he had known Bacon a long time and he had a working knowledge of how the lieutenant's mind functioned. He had expected this reaction and so, pretending that he had no intention of arguing the point, he tapped his rolled-up prints against his calf. Certain now of Bacon's attention, he tucked the roll under one arm and strolled toward the door.

"Just thought I'd ask," he said indifferently.

Bacon stopped him in the doorway.

"Wait a minute!" he said, his gray gaze suspicious. "What've you got there?"

"What do you care?"

"If it's got anything to do with murder I care plenty."

"Who said it had."

"Don't get smart with me," Bacon said. "You don't come in here wanting a deal without having something to make a deal with."

Murdock shrugged and moved back with an outward display of reluctance. He sat down and slipped the elastic from the prints. He took his time rolling them the other way to straighten them out, seeing Bacon's impatience mount and hearing him say: "Come on, come on." When he offered the prints he got ready for Bacon's blast and presently it came.

Bacon glanced at the top print, stared, then fanned the rest of them out. Still busy with his inspection he said, more exasperated than angry:

"Why, God damn you, Murdock! You had these all the time."

"No."

"Then how'd you get 'em? Somebody slip them under your door?"

"Do you want to know or would you rather hear yourself talk?" Murdock said, and then he was explaining what had happened to the negatives after he had made them. He spoke of Walt Carey and his failure to put the negatives in Murdock's desk that first afternoon. He said that Brady had never seen them because they had not been in the desk when he called for them.

"I didn't get them until last night," he said. "It was so late when I finished making prints I went to bed—you'd already gone home then—and this morning I hardly had a chance to look at them when you called me and told me about Denham."

"Okay, okay," Bacon said, still more interested in the new-found evidence than in Murdock's explanation. "These check out on Denham-Danton. They give us possible motives for Arthur Enders and Gloria Alderson and the son, Jerry. But it's that dame, Rita, that we'll talk to first."

"When you find her."

"Don't worry, we will."

"Give me a half hour with her first and I'll tell you where she is now."

"You'll tell me anyway," Bacon said bristling.

Murdock looked back at him, his dark gaze steady. "Will I?" he said quietly.

Bacon swung his chair round, a flush working on his thin face. "What the hell's the matter with you?" he shouted. "We've got men out now. It's just a question of time— maybe fifteen minutes, maybe an hour. But you want to horn in first, is that it? So the *Courier* can get a beat?"

He had other things to say, some of them unpleasant, and Murdock sat there, his temper in hand because he understood how it was with Bacon. Bacon was a cop and he had to play according to the rule book; he had to argue against any abrogation of such rules and he did so now until he ran out of words.

"I didn't have to come here," Murdock said, still quiet. "I didn't have to give you those prints—at least not now. I didn't have to tell you I knew where Rita Alderson was, did I? If I had what it takes to wrap this up I'd put it in your lap and you know it. You know why, too. Because Tom Brady was a friend of mine; a damn sight better friend of mine than he was of yours. Right now I'm not even working for the *Courier*, at least not officially, and the only reason I've been sticking my neck out is because I wanted to help."

The quiet sincerity of Murdock's words took the edge off Bacon's asperity and counteracted his complaints. For a brief moment he had a sheepish air but he was not ready to admit that he was wrong.

"You never tried to play cop with me before," he said.

"I'm not trying to now."

"But you want to get to Rita Alderson before we do."

"I could be there now, couldn't I?"

"Yeah, I guess you could at that," Bacon said, and sighed loudly. "So why did you come here? I still don't get it."

"I think I can get more out of her than you can. You bring her down here and maybe she'll talk and maybe she won't. She'll talk to me because I know her." He hesitated, remembering the reports but knowing that nothing could be gained by mentioning them. "Give me a chance and then you can walk in and take over."

"Talking to you alone won't do much good. She can deny anything she tells you unless you've got a witness."

"I'll have one."

"Who?"

"Frank Kirby. I'm picking him up at four."

"You've got it all figured out, hunh?" Bacon said sardonically.

"No," Murdock said. "I'm playing this one by ear and hoping."

"Okay," Bacon said resignedly. "But there's no deal. Officially I get a tip on where the dame is and I go there at four thirty to pick her up for questioning, right?"

"Right."

"Where is she?"

"At the Harvey House," Murdock said, and mentioned the room number.

Bacon still looked doubtful, but having committed himself he glanced at his watch and said Murdock had better get going.

"Just play it cozy, huh?" he said. "You can do your talking but let me be the cop."

Murdock said he intended to do just that but as he rode down in the elevator he knew there was one more thing to be done. Because he did not want to walk in on Rita Alderson without giving her some warning and a chance to prepare herself, he stopped on the main floor to telephone her. When he had his connection, he said what he had to say, though this took longer than he had expected because he had to explain that he was not coming to see her just to be sociable.

Frank Kirby was standing in the doorway of his office building when Murdock drove up five minutes later. He looked very natty in his pin-striped suit and gray hat, but when he slid in beside Murdock his gray-green eyes were attentive under the upward slanting brows.

"What's up?" he said. "Where're we going?"

"To have a talk with Rita Alderson."

"Ahh," said Kirby. "That's your lead, hunh? You think she ties in with the Denham job?"

Murdock spoke of the prints he had given Bacon. He did not mention the reports but the things he said were based in part on what Tom Brady had written. He repeated the things Bacon had said about Denham. He said Denham's real name was Benjamin Danton and a copy of a marriage license proved that he had married a girl named Ruth Colby.

"Rita Carr was a stage name Ruth Colby took," he said.

"Do you know that or are you guessing?"

"I know it."

"Then this half-brother business was a phony," Kirby said. "The guy was actually Rita Alderson's first husband."

"There may be more to it than that," Murdock said. "Brady went to Mexico to follow up on Danton. Before that he checked in California and Nevada to see if a divorce had ever been granted to Danton or Ruth Colby. He couldn't find any such record. He brought back a letter from an attorney in Mexico City. The attorney had made a search there and in Juarez, and the letter I photographed said that to the best of his knowledge no Mexican divorce had been granted either."

Kirby swore softly as the meaning of this statement became clear. "Then that could mean she was maybe never legally married to George Alderson." He hesitated, watching Murdock now and his voice thoughtful.

"How come you know so much about those photographs all of a sudden. I thought you couldn't remember what was on those documents."

Murdock repeated his story of the negatives and how he had found them. He said he wanted to talk to Rita before the police did because he thought, with what he now knew, he could get the truth out of her.

21

THE Harvey House was a residential hotel that specialized in long-term tenants and did very little in the way of transient business. Eminently respectable, it was not the sort of establishment that would occur to anyone as a place to hide out, which may have explained why Bacon's men had not yet located Rita Alderson.

Her room was a corner one, spacious and high ceilinged, with a connecting door in one wall so that it could be used as part of a suite when necessary. The walls were thick, the construction sturdy, and the locks old fashioned so that a key had to be used on the inside in order to unlock the door. The click of that key answered Murdock's knock, and when the knob turned he pushed forward, Kirby at his heels.

He saw the look of surprise on the girl's face when she saw Kirby, but Murdock moved quickly past her, eyes busy as they sized up the room, his camera in one hand and the other working on the case he had slung over his shoulder. He noticed the heavy double bed, the chest, the bureau, the one easy chair, the love seat which had been placed between the two windows. Holding the case slightly in front of him so that his back shielded his movements, he started the recording mechanism and withdrew the small microphone so that it extended two or three inches over the outside of the case. Then he put the case on the floor at the end of the love seat, turning it so the end with the microphone was toward the wall where it could not be seen by anyone in the room. He placed the camera beside it. When he straightened he was ready for Rita.

She still wore the gabardine skirt, well wrinkled now and no longer neat, and the cashmere sweater. Her face looked drawn and paler than usual so that her cheekbones were accented and the dark-blue eyes seemed more shadowed and withdrawn. Now she could not keep them still and they darted from Murdock to Kirby and back again as Murdock picked up a newspaper that had been tossed down beside the easy chair. When he saw that it was an afternoon edition he knew she had read about Denham.

"How's your head?" he said.

"My what?"

"Your head. Last night when you came to my place you had a bruise on it. . . . Right about here," he added, as he put his finger to a spot high on one side of his forehead.

She was eyeing him warily now and Kirby's gaze was narrowed and speculative.

"She came to see you last night?" he said. "What time was that?"

"Between one thirty and two," Murdock said and explained how the girl had passed out on his divan. "All right to use the telephone?" he said to her, moving toward it and not waiting for a reply. "You'd better sit down, Rita," he said. "This may take quite a while."

He watched her move over to the love seat and by then he had located the slip of paper on which he had written the number of the night barman at Freddie's Bar. This time a man's voice answered and Murdock identified himself. He said he was trying to check on a girl who had been there the night before.

"A good-looking blonde," he said, "in a camel's-hair coat. She was drinking alone and was there right up to closing."

"What about her?" the man said.

"I wondered if you remembered her."

"Sure."

"What time did she come in?"

"Around eleven thirty. . . . No, it was before that. Maybe around eleven fifteen."

"Did she stay until closing?"

"She sure did. We had to argue with her to get her out then."

Murdock thanked him and hung up. He went over and sat down beside the girl and Kirby took the easy chair.

"I found the reports, Rita," he said, and heard the small sucking sound as she drew in a quick breath. "I talked Harriett into letting me take a look at your room. . . . How come you kept them?"

She did not make an immediate reply and he saw that her head was down, that her hands seemed braced on the cushion on either side of her hips. When she lifted her chin she had to toss her head to get the blonde hair out of her eyes.

"I don't know," she said finally. "I didn't know what to do. I was afraid to destroy them and afraid not to."

Murdock could understand this much, but because he had to feel his way along he was not quite sure what he should say next. Somehow the confidence that had been a vital part of his idea had suddenly dissipated and he began to wonder whether he had done the right thing by coming here.

"I gave them to Harriett," he said, "because she's going to have to pay for them. But I read them first. I also have copies of the pictures I took of Brady's documents. I can understand why you were so worried that first afternoon when you were waiting for me outside the paper. . . . That was quite a story you told me yesterday afternoon," he said. "About your childhood and career and marriage."

"It was true," she said with sudden spirit.

"Not all of it. You forgot to admit that your real name is Ruth Colby. Brady worked backwards on that one. Harriett was suspicious of Denham and Brady went out to California and started checking on a girl named Rita Carr who was a part-time actress. From friends of hers he found out what her right name was and he got a copy of your birth certificate. He found out you married a Benjamin Danton. There was no record of a divorce but you told George Alderson—"

"I thought I was divorced," she protested.

"That's easy enough to say now."

"It's true. What I told you about my husband beating me and going to jail and all that."

"This was Benjamin Danton—Barry Denham?"

"Yes. I told him I was going to get a divorce and he said I needn't bother. He said he'd had enough too. He was going to Mexico and he'd get the divorce there and I could save my money. About a month after that I got a wire from him. I remember every word of it. 'Divorce in the works,' it said. 'From now on you're on your own.' Why shouldn't I believe that?" she demanded. "Wouldn't you?"

Murdock waited and she said: "I never saw him again until he came here. He'd been working in Mexico all that time and he got in some trouble and had to leave. He went to Los Angeles to look for me and he found out I'd gone to Ogunquit. When he got that far he discovered I was married. He came here and telephoned me. He said there never had been a divorce, that I was not George's legal wife at all."

"George didn't leave a will," Murdock said. "Without one you stood to inherit everything. At least the hundred and fifty thousand his father left him; probably more."

Kirby, who had been listening to every word, cleared his throat, his voice blunt.

"All Denham had to do was open his mouth and you wouldn't get a dime," he said to her. "Who thought up that phony business of the new name and the unemployed actor routine?"

Rita's head came down again and this time she spoke with her eyes averted.

"I did. Not the name. He'd already been using that. But there had to be some reason why he should come here. I had to give some explanation to the family and then I thought of all the summer theaters in Maine and on the Cape. I thought if he pretended to be an actor it would sound all right. I couldn't say he was a brother because of the name, so I did the next best thing."

"So he made a deal with you," Kirby said. "He told you he'd keep still until you got the estate money if you cut him in. How much did he want?"

"Half." She looked up and continued quickly. "But that's not the reason I had to do what he said. It wasn't the money."

"Oh, no?" Kirby said with heavy irony.

"No. George was always generous. I had a little money. I had all the clothes I needed and my engagement ring and two or three pieces of jewelry that were good—presents he'd given me. . . . It was Jerry," she said, and turned to Murdock, her eyes asking for his understanding.

"You know how we felt about each other. He wanted to

marry me and I wanted it too, because I love him. Even Barry could see that when he came to the house that time. He guessed the rest. He said I could keep still and he would too. When I got the estate I could pay him and he'd get a divorce and no one would ever know the truth. He said if I didn't want to play his way he'd not only tell Harriett to make sure I got nothing, but he would never give me a divorce so Jerry and I could get married."

This much Murdock believed because he had seen enough of this girl to know that her moods and actions were motivated by her feelings rather than by a calculating brain. Neither her background nor her training had given her the mental equipment to match wits with the world and this may have been the reason why George Alderson had married her in the first place. For George was tired of sophisticates and he had responded not only to the fine body and the tawny attractiveness of her face and the striking eyes, but to some other quality that was young and ingenuous and not yet tarnished by the sort of café society he knew so well. And so, unable to outthink Denham, she had been trapped by her emotions and in the end she would have to pay the piper.

Now, indicating the newspaper on the floor, Murdock asked if she had read about her first husband. He said he had a theory about how Denham had been killed.

"You went to his room last night. That's where you got the bruise, wasn't it? Why?"

"I told him I couldn't go on any longer. I told him I was afraid, that it would only be a question of time before the police found out the truth." She rearranged her hands on the cushions and glanced up. "He was furious," she said. "He hit me. He said if I told the truth now I'd wind up in the electric chair."

"You went out before he did," Murdock said. "He got a call from someone. He took a gun which means he was ready for trouble. So here's what I think happened. You knew where he kept his car, didn't you?"

"Yes."

"At that time of night, with one attendant and no fence around the lot, it would be easy enough to move in and climb into the back seat of the right car. After that you could simply wait until Denham came along. When he drove to the right place all you'd have to do would be to put a gun to the back of his head and tell him to stop. It would be easy enough then to get his gun and make that one close-up shot. When it was over you could fix the doors so he'd be locked in. . . . Oh, yes, and push the body on the floor so it wouldn't be noticed for a while."

"No." She shook her head violently, her long lashes high. Her red mouth was open and she closed it. "No. I didn't."

"I didn't say you did," Murdock said. "If the barman at Freddie's Bar told the truth—he says you came in about a quarter after eleven, which was the time Denham left the hotel, and stayed there—you couldn't have done it. But I'm not much interested in Denham, Rita. I think that's how it happened. I don't know how to prove it. I'm not going to try.

"It's different with Brady," he said. "You were there. A tenant saw you in the lobby at nine o'clock. He can identify you once the police pick you up. You took the briefcase and Brady's reports and you never could have done that if he had been alive. To get those reports from a man like Brady you'd have to kill—"

"No."

"I say yes. So will a jury."

For another moment she hesitated, her eyes wide open

as she stared back at him. Then, as though she had reached some decision of her own, her hand moved between the cushions. When it came up it held the automatic and her body twisted as she tried to pull away to give herself room.

This time Murdock was ready. He had expected some such attempt and he moved when she did, reaching out with one hand, leaning forward, then striking sharply at her wrist.

It was all over in two seconds and she never had a chance. He heard her cry out as he hit her hand and the force of the blow sent the gun spinning to one side. It struck the carpet five feet away, turned over once, and came to rest not far from Kirby's chair.

For another moment or two there was no sound but the small whimper from the girl as she rubbed her bruised wrist. Until then Kirby had remained motionless, nothing moving but his eyes. Narrowed and suspicious now beneath the angling brows, they took time to study the girl before he leaned forward without leaving his chair and retrieved the automatic. Holding it loosely, his hand dangling between his knees, he fixed his gaze on Murdock, as though waiting for him to continue.

Murdock leaned back and let his breath out softly, aware that the first act was over. He had learned what he had to know about the girl's past and her motives, but there was more to come. He was not quite sure how it would develop but he knew it was too late to turn back now. He had set this up and he had to keep calling the shots. It was his move and as he considered the consequences he felt the beginning of some pressure inside him, as though a hidden valve had been opened by some mechanism of the mind.

"You're going to have to convince the police pretty soon, Rita," he said. "You might as well start rehearsing. . . .

How did you know Brady was going to ask me to make some copies for him?"

She was still stroking her wrist, her head down and the blonde hair obscuring her eyes. When she spoke her voice was muffled.

"I overheard him when he telephoned Harriett."

"You heard him say he was going to have certain documents put on film and that I was going to make the copies. That scared you so much you came to the *Courier* to ask if I would let you know what I was photographing."

"I didn't stop to think or I never would have asked. I was upset. I didn't know what to do and—"

"All right," Murdock cut in. "And so you went to Brady's office at nine that night."

"Yes."

"Why?"

"He telephoned me." She pushed her hair back and looked up. "At dinner time. He said he would be busy that evening but if I could come to his office at nine he'd like to talk to me."

Murdock weighed the words and found them reasonable. For Brady's letter to his daughter indicated that he was worried about the trouble he would make with his report. He had known the truth about Ruth Colby and Rita Alderson and he had probably wanted to give her a little warning of what was to come.

"So you went there. With that gun?" he said, pointing to the automatic Kirby held.

"No. There wasn't any gun," she said, the words tumbling out now in her effort to explain. "I went up and knocked and there was no answer, so I went in. He was there on the floor. I didn't know he was dead," she said, her voice rising. "I didn't know what had happened at first; I didn't know what to do."

"Go on," Murdock said as she took a breath.

"I went over and spoke to him. I tried to shake him and then I saw the stain on his shirt. I seemed to know then that he must be dead and—oh, I don't know what I thought," she said. "I was too frightened to think. I was petrified and all I could think of was that I should get out."

"Did you see a gun?"

"No. But I did see the sheets of paper on the desk, clipped together. I don't know how I made myself take time to look at them but I did. Then I saw this was the report he was going to turn in the next day and I knew what it would mean. . . . I took it," she said with a show of defiance. "I didn't stop to think whether I should or not, I just did. I got all the way to the door before I realized there would be other copies."

"The file cabinet was open?"

"Yes. And because I was afraid to take the time to look— I couldn't be sure how many copies there were—I knew I had to take everything. When I looked round and saw the briefcase I took it."

"Did you go through Brady's pockets?"

"No. I—I couldn't have done it."

"Or his raincoat?"

"No. I told you what I did," she cried. "I took the papers and the briefcase and—"

Murdock cut her off. "All right," he said. "So when did Kirby get in touch with you?"

She started to reply and then stopped. She gave Kirby a furtive glance and caught the edge of her lower lip between her teeth.

"The next morning," she said finally.

"He telephoned you?"

"Yes. He asked me to meet him downtown. I did."

"What did he say?"

"He said he knew I was Ruth Colby, that I had never been divorced. He said he was willing to keep quiet about it until I got my inheritance if I'd pay."

"How much?"

"A third."

Having studiously ignored Kirby's presence, Murdock now looked at the detective and Kirby looked back at him. He had not moved either his body or the gun, but the gray-green eyes had hard glints in them now and his mouth was tight.

"How did you know Rita was Ruth Colby?"

"Who says I did—besides her?" He glanced at the girl.

Murdock ignored the remark. "One thing I do know and that is that Brady didn't tell you or show you that report. Brady had a very strong feeling about the confidential nature of his work. Which has to mean that either you had a look at the report, or part of it, or at the originals of the documents I photographed—Brady had them with him when he left me at the studio—or both."

Kirby's mouth dipped at one corner and his quick laugh made an unpleasant sound.

"You're pressing, chum," he said. "She says I propositioned her and I say no. She's the one that took the reports, not me."

Murdock's dark gaze remained steady as he put his thoughts in order. The pressure was still there inside him, not bad yet but building. When he spoke he took his time.

"How would you know she took the reports unless you saw her, Kirby?"

"What the hell. She just admitted she took 'em."

"But you called her the morning after the murder."

"That's what she says."

"Actually, I think you did see her take the reports. I think she trapped you there and if she hadn't been lucky—or if you hadn't been quick—you'd have had to kill her too."

"What are you," Kirby said, "psychic?"

"The physical facts of that killing don't fit a woman."

"Don't they?"

"And since we're just kicking this around suppose I do a little guessing," Murdock said. "Let's start with the initial supposition that was made the first night. Because Brady was killed with his own gun we decided that someone, maybe a woman, had come in and covered him. This some-one demanded the reports but Brady would not take a thing like that sitting still. So he eased his gun out of that drawer and was seen doing so. He was forced to put it on the desk. The killer took it and when he was ready he used it."

"So?"

"If that had happened that drawer would never have been jerked out on the floor. The drawer would have been eased open an inch at a time, and just enough so Brady could get his hand on the gun. To jerk at the drawer, to make any sudden move, would be stupid and Brady was never stupid about a gun; he had too much experience."

He paused and when Kirby made no comment, he said: "I think the killer jerked that drawer open to get at a gun he knew was there. If you don't mind my guessing I think it happened like this. I think you had a key to Brady's file. You had a reputation for being ambitious and hotheaded and you were in business to make money. You were hoping for a big score and you knew Brady had a nice assignment.

I think you got curious when he told you he was taking the precaution of having some papers copied by me.

"I think you were in the office, not expecting him back from Kelleher's so soon. I think you were giving those reports a once-over and he caught you at it. If he did and you gave him any argument I think he took a poke at you. His coat was on the floor where he dropped it. He took his swing—you were behind the desk—and he knocked you over the chair and when you landed on your back you came down on the wastebasket, overturning it and bending the top with your weight. That drawer was right there in your corner and you yanked it open because you had to hurry and you came up with his gun."

Again Murdock hesitated, a little out of breath now and conscious of some new pressure that began to expand as the word picture he had drawn became clearer. The early tension was still with him, but this had to do with the situation he had made and the dangerous potential that was now a part of it.

But his early bitterness, which had been born of a helpless rage and his sense of personal loss, had dissipated somewhat during the past day. Now the feeling came back to him in increasing strength. It showed in the hard line of his jaw, in the narrowed brightness of his eyes. For he looked at Frank Kirby now not as a detective but as the man who had killed his friend. It was no longer easy to sit and wait while he spoke of things that would prove his point, but because there was no other way he tried to think clearly and keep his voice controlled.

"I don't know why you pulled the trigger," he said. "It's not important now. But I think you were standing there with Brady's gun in your hand when Rita knocked on the door. I guess that knock saved her," he said. "Because you

must have known that if you were caught you'd have to
kill again.

"You had one chance," he said. "The little conference
room. You made it before she came in and you had to wait
there until she left. You had to let her take the reports, but
she didn't know about the original documents that Brady
had and you got them from his coat pocket. You probably
still have them, someplace. When you were sure she was
on her way you put the gun on the floor, called police headquarters, and sat down to wait."

He stopped then, feeling the dampness at his palms and
the pull at his muscles as he sat waiting for Kirby and keeping one eye on the gun.

"That's quite a yarn," Kirby said. "That's a lot of guessing but without some evidence—and I haven't heard any
yet—it don't add up. The grand jury wouldn't give that
routine a tumble and you know it."

"I've got a little evidence." Murdock leaned forward and
shifted his weight. "But that part is not for me. Let's get the
police in on it and see what Lieutenant Bacon thinks."

He made his move to stand up as he spoke but before he
could rise he saw Kirby's hand snap upward. That stopped
him and he stayed that way, half crouching, as the automatic leveled at him and Kirby's lips flattened.

"Sit still!" Kirby said coldly. "Just relax. Let's hear this
evidence, hunh? Now that we're all so cozy let's get it all."

He shifted his weight slightly, the tendons in the back
of his hand tightening as Murdock hesitated. When he saw
Murdock ease down on the love seat he nodded approv-
ingly.

22

WHEN Kent Murdock leaned back against the cushions he felt the pressure of Rita's shoulder against his own and was glad she was sitting on his right away from Kirby. He turned to look at her aslant, his smile crooked in an effort to reassure her. He was not sure it did any good because her face was pale and tight across the cheekbones, the dark-blue eyes enormous and bright with apprehension. Because there was nothing he could say to her then, he turned back to Kirby.

"For one thing," he said, "there's the smudge on the back of that raincoat of yours I have in my closet."

Kirby scowled and was instantly attentive. "What?"

"I didn't know our raincoats had been switched at the Aldersons'," Murdock said. "But I saw the smudge on the back of the one I had when I hung it up that night. It annoyed me because I'd recently had it cleaned. I thought I got it when I threw the coat in the back of the car at Aldersons' and then I remembered I'd used it as a pillow for Walt Carey's head when I found him unconscious earlier. This afternoon when I began to get some ideas I took a good look."

"Ideas?" Kirby said irritably. "You mean you brought me up here to—"

"I wanted to get the two of you together and see what happened."

Kirby understood that much and he did not like it.

"You'll find out," he said viciously, "but good. What about the coat?"

"That smudge looks bluish," Murdock said. "It looks as if it could have been made by a typewriter ribbon. The police have still got the one they took from Brady's basket. They should be able to tell."

The gleam in those gray-green eyes had a feral quality now and the pressure of Kirby's jaws made them white at the corners. He spoke between his teeth.

"What else?"

"You said you had seen a woman come out of your building while you were standing in a doorway to get out of the rain. I don't know why you told me unless it was because you wanted me to think you were playing along with me. You knew the police were already looking for such a woman, so it couldn't do much harm."

"What about it?"

"It was a lie. You didn't see any woman come out. You were never out in the rain." Murdock leaned forward, his phrases quick. "When I sat down in the office to wait I folded your coat and put it on the floor. It wasn't wet like mine. That neat gray felt of yours didn't have a single rain spot. You were in the office when the rain hit at nine o'clock, Kirby," he said. "The only time you went out was when you left with Bacon and me."

Nothing changed in Kirby's face except the color and when there was no reply, Murdock said:

"Unless you were calling on someone in that building you were in your office from before nine until nine-o-seven when you phoned the police. Doing what, Kirby? . . . You ducked into the little conference room when Rita knocked. You had to stay there and watch her walk off with the reports but there were still the original documents in Brady's coat. Did you get them? Did you put them in an envelope and drop them in the mailbox in the lobby before you phoned? What about those two thugs you hired to look for the negatives I'd made? When did you call them?

"You knew Rita had the reports," he said, "and that didn't worry you because you had the original documents. But there were still those negatives to worry about. Once they came to light you had no pitch to make and nothing to collect from Rita or anyone else because the secret would come out. I can understand why you sent those two punks to my place, but why did they bother Sally Fisher?"

"I had to be sure," Kirby said. "When Brady came back from your office that afternoon I asked if he got his negatives and he said you were to leave them in your desk. He said if he didn't pick them up he'd ask the girl to. I found the originals on him but no negatives. I had to figure she might have taken the envelope home with her."

Murdock understood it now, just as he remembered how he and Bacon had discarded the possibility that it might have been Kirby who had hired the two. They had reasoned it out and it had seemed an acceptable premise at the time because, lacking some facts, they had drawn the wrong conclusion.

"You phoned them from your office, didn't you?" he said. "Before you called the police. It was the only time you could have phoned them. I guess they must have owed you something from the days when you were a cop."

Kirby did not deny this. Instead he began to curse in savage tones, at Murdock first, and then at Brady.

"He walked in on me like he always walked," Kirby said. "Not making a sound. I looked up and there he was. I hadn't even finished reading the report. When he saw what I was doing he blew his stack, the silly stupe. He grabbed them and I tried to argue with him. I told him he could collect fifty grand from the dame"—he glanced at Rita—"if he'd just hold out a little on the old woman. He swung at me and missed and then he nailed me good."

He leaned forward and now his jacket gaped open and Murdock saw the strap that anchored the shoulder holster. Then, because Murdock was not quite finished, he said, his contempt obvious:

"You couldn't take it, hunh? You were quick on the trigger when you were a cop and you never changed."

"Nobody does that to me and gets away with it," Kirby said. "Sure I grabbed for the drawer. I got up with the gun. The crazy fool tried to take it away from me, and that's where he made his mistake."

Murdock let his breath out slowly, sick inside as the picture came to him and tormented by some odd desire born of rage and bitterness and, perhaps, vindictiveness. Because the reaction was so foreign to his nature he held it in check, reminding himself that there was a little more to be done.

"You're the guy I walked in on at Brady's apartment. You had to be sure there was nothing there that could spoil your plan."

"I should have dropped you then," Kirby said. "It would have saved me the trouble of doing it now."

"And Denham," Murdock said. "He nearly took care of you, didn't he?" He turned to glance at Rita, who seemed not to have moved a muscle. "You told him about Kirby, didn't you?"

She bobbed her head, her voice a whisper. "I had to. I was afraid not to."

"Maybe Denham had the right idea," Murdock said to Kirby. "He didn't want you cutting in and he missed you by only a couple of inches."

Kirby swore again. "But he missed."

"And you took care of him because you didn't want to cut him in on the profits."

Kirby's answering grunt was a dry, contemptuous sound. "Think again," he said. "You're slipping with your guesses. Denham had a gun and he thought he was big time. I could tell by looking at him—so could Bacon, I'll bet—that he was a mean one. I was cutting in on him and he didn't like it. He figured they'd never get him for dumping me so he tried."

He grunted again and cleared his throat. "Maybe the money was an angle but it wasn't important," he said. "When a guy is gunning for you and you can't yell for protection you haven't got much choice. You're his target all the time. I could wait until Denham found his chance to take another shot at me or I could go to him first. . . . There was nothing to it," he said.

"I phoned him and made a date. I said we should talk it over because there was enough for both of us. I knew he'd take his car and I knew he'd come with a gun. He did, with me hiding in back just like you figured. The gun was right there on the seat beside him. All I had to do after I jammed my own gun against the back of his neck was lean over and pick it up."

Murdock swallowed and started to get up. What he wanted would now be on tape and as he came slowly to his feet he looked at the automatic in Kirby's hand. It had never worried him because he had unloaded it the night before and there had been no extra bullets in Rita's handbag.

He watched Kirby rise and get his balance and when he saw the brightness in that pale and narrowed gaze he knew that Kirby would not hesitate to shoot. For himself all he had to do was cover five feet before Kirby knew the gun was empty and what he wanted most was to get his hands on the man responsible for Tom Brady's death.

The bitterness was spreading through him now and he no longer had to contain it. He could feel the slight tremor in his knees. When he spoke his voice was shaking.

"What are you going to do with the gun?" he said.

"Use it. What the hell do you think? On you and on her. It's her gun, ain't it? So let the cops figure it."

"Okay," Murdock said and let his weight come forward. "Use it. And what're you going to do when you find out it—"

Murdock was moving as he spoke. He had it all worked out. He was sure he had the time he needed. That his plan went awry and erupted in unexpected violence was not his fault; for though he had weighed the tangibles and found them to his liking he could not forecast the future nor could he prevent fate, in the form of Lieutenant Bacon, from taking a hand.

It was not that Murdock had forgotten Bacon. He had glanced at the hall door from time to time and it would not have surprised him to see it open now. But Bacon had been dealt a hand and he had played it the way that seemed best to him. For the door that swung open as Murdock spoke came not from the hall but from the connecting room.

Murdock heard it before he saw it because he stood sideways at that door. He had no chance to finish the sentence, to tell Kirby that the automatic he held was not loaded, and in later years there were times when he wondered whether he would have finished the sentence even if there had been time.

But in that first instant his momentum carried him toward the man and the gun. That was all he had in mind until he saw Kirby step back and hesitate as though selecting his target; then, ignoring Murdock, he swung the gun toward Bacon and Sergeant Keogh.

They both yelled at the same time. They said: "Drop it!"

Both had guns in their hands, but it was Keogh who fired when Kirby squeezed the trigger and then yanked hard at it. Had the automatic been loaded, Kirby would have had the first shot, since his mind was already made up, but now it was Keogh, no killer by choice, who fired, aiming low so that his slug slammed into Kirby's thigh, twisting him instantly and then knocking the leg from under him.

He hit the floor at an awkward angle, the automatic dropping as he fell. By then Murdock had slid to a stop. After that there was no time left and he could only stare in helpless horror as Kirby rolled and came to his good knee with his own short-barreled revolver in his hand.

Bacon yelled again and so did Murdock, though he was not aware of it. Even the girl cried out some protest. All went unheeded as Kirby, ignoring the odds and driven by some compulsion beyond his control, completed his turn. Then, his mind triggered by desperation or by some ingrown characteristic that had made him so handy with a gun in the past, he fired.

So did Bacon and Keogh.

The three shots came almost like a volley to rock the room with sound, but it was a ragged volley, one shot—Kirby's—coming a split instant too late.

And this time the two policemen knew the score. They had to play for keeps and they stood there as the sound died away, watching Kirby fold over on his knee and tip slowly on his side.

Murdock did not see him collapse. He was watching Bacon and Keogh holster their guns, seeing now the man who stood behind them and understanding at last how this had come about.

For the third man was a headquarters specialist named Jansen. His field was electronics and wire-tapping and he still held a headset in one hand. How long the three had been in the other room was unimportant now, but, remembering the time he had taken to telephone Rita, Murdock knew that Bacon could have taken his station first. Bacon had given the half hour he had promised, but Bacon was a professional and he had played his cards accordingly.

Now he and Keogh moved back from the twisted figure on the floor. Bacon collected the two guns and Keogh jerked the counterpane from the bed and spread it over the body. By that time Bacon was ready for Murdock.

"You wanted to play it your way, hunh?" he said, his tone testy with reaction. "You would have stopped one for sure, going for the gun the way you did, if we hadn't decided it was time to crash in." He hesitated, frowning down at the automatic. "It must've jammed," he said. "He might have nailed one of us if it hadn't."

"It's empty."

Bacon did not believe him. He pulled back the slide to make sure. He looked up, brows bent and gray eyes cloudy with bewilderment.

"You knew it," he said finally. "That's why you—" He let the sentence hang and tried again. "He never had a chance," he said.

"He had a chance," Murdock said. "He could have settled for a slug in the leg. He didn't have to go for his own gun. And anyway," he said bluntly, "he killed Tom Brady, didn't he?"

"Yeah," Bacon said, thoughtful now. "That's right, he did."

"He asked for what he got," Murdock said. "Forget it." He turned then to get his midget recorder. He turned it off and brought it back to Bacon. "How much did you get?" he asked.

"All of it," Bacon said. "We got here before you did. We had a bug on the door."

"All right, now you've got two sets," Murdock said and opened the instrument to wind the tape and remove the cartridge. By that time Bacon wanted to know more.

"I still don't get it," he said. "How did you know the gun was empty?" He listened as Murdock explained and then said: "But why did she"—he glanced at the girl—"try to use it here?"

"I told her to."

"What?"

Murdock hesitated as he put his thoughts in order. He knew it would not be easy to make Bacon understand, but he had to try.

"I telephoned her before I came."

He glanced round and found Rita still sitting on the love seat, her young face white with shock and an odd blankness in her gaze. Because he wanted to help her, he went to her and took her hands in his.

"It's all right," he said, hoping that if he could make her talk she would feel better. "It's the best way. Tell the Lieutenant what I told you over the telephone."

She blinked the long lashes and her eyes focused. "He said the police were looking for me and that he was coming over to give me a chance to talk. He said my only chance was to tell the truth even if he put the pressure on me." She swallowed and said: "He asked me if I still had the gun and I said yes. He said to have it hidden somewhere handy so I could get it out in a hurry. He said when he accused me of killing Mr. Brady, when he used the word jury, I was to yank the gun out as if I was going to use it on him. I didn't understand him and I said so and he said not to argue; to do what he said because it was my only chance."

She stopped, out of breath and still bewildered but with color beginning to tint her cheeks.

"I still don't get it," Bacon said sourly. "It was a frame but—"

"Look," Murdock said. "I was sure Kirby was our man. I had a little evidence—you heard it—but I didn't think it was enough. The only way to get what we needed was to make him talk. He was carrying a gun of his own; I knew that. Being the kind of guy he was I figured that when I crowded him, when he saw I had enough for an indictment, he'd pull that gun. He sure as hell wouldn't talk, or confess to anything, unless he was sure he was in the driver's seat. To make him talk I had to give him a gun and let him think—"

"Yeah," said Bacon. "That much I see. So you gave him the empty gun."

"I knocked it right at his feet," Murdock said. "I knew he'd pick it up. And don't forget, when Rita pulled the gun I was making it look as though I thought she was the guilty one, as though she pulled it because she was trapped. Once Kirby had the gun I had to hope he wouldn't realize what had happened. I had to count on one thing."

"What?"

"That he had murder on his mind. Just like Denham when he waited for Kirby earlier last night. Twice before Kirby had killed men with their own guns, and here it was again. If he thought he had to shoot he would be a lot safer using her gun than his own." He shrugged, his grin twisted and humorless. "Of course, if he'd started to examine it I would have had to jump him and take my chances. The way I felt about Brady I figured I could do all right."

"You generally do," Bacon said. "Though I'll be damned if I know why. . . . Okay," he said with a sigh of resignation. "What the hell am I arguing about? It worked. . . . Go ahead, get your picture."

"It's the only thing that'll be exclusive for the *Courier*," Murdock said, "because it's too late for the afternoon final and too early for the morning bulldog. This time you do the talking to the press. I don't know anything about anything. Okay?"

Bacon studied him a moment, gray eyes half open and busy before he nodded. "Okay," he said, and turned to start giving orders to Keogh and Jansen.

It was nearly ten o'clock when Kent Murdock came into his office and slumped wearily down in his desk chair. The session at headquarters with Bacon, assorted brass, and an assistant district attorney had been both protracted and repetitious. Coffee and sandwiches had been served to sustain the participants and in the end no specific charges were filed against Rita Alderson, pending an additional hearing.

Arthur Enders, as the family attorney, had appeared with Jerry Alderson to make the proper assurances, and when Rita and Jerry left together Murdock got the idea from the way they looked at each other that it mattered very little to either of them that Rita had never been legally married to George and would not therefore inherit anything from his estate.

Murdock was glad about that because he realized what she had gone through during the past days, but he could not forget that there would be a funeral the following morning and now his dark eyes were brooding and his mood was black. Presently he knew he would lock up and go forth in search of two or three drinks, or maybe four or five, depending upon how he felt at the time. For he needed a lift, even an artificial one, and he felt he was entitled to it. All he needed was the energy to get himself out of the building and while he was waiting for the proper moment the telephone rang.

"Kent?" a woman's voice said. "This is Harriett Alderson."

"Oh?" said Murdock, who could not have been more surprised. "Well, hello."

"Arthur Enders has just left," she said. "He told me what happened."

Murdock said: "Oh?" again because it was all he could think of.

"I've been thinking a lot since this afternoon," she said. "Nobody has talked to me the way you did in years. I resented every word of it until I realized it was the truth. It helped enormously."

Murdock, a little embarrassed now, said he was glad.

"I haven't too many years left but I don't think it's ever too late to make a change for the better, do you? . . . And I was wondering—are you terribly busy? Could you come over for a drink?"

Murdock cleared his throat and stammered and she helped him out.

"Jerry and Rita are out somewhere. So are Gloria and Donald. It's the first time they've been out together in I don't know when. You see I talked to them and I think it's

done some good. So there's only Henderson,"—her laugh
came softly—"and I can't talk to him, can I?"

"Well—" Murdock said, his eyes no longer brooding.

"I can offer you twelve-year-old Scotch and if you're
hungry I'm sure Henderson can whip up something. . . .
For a little while? Just to talk. I—I could use a little more
help if you have time."

The quiet sincerity of her words moved Murdock
strangely, not only because they were unexpected but because he understood that for anyone heretofore so proud
and imperious her need must be very real.

And now, a grin beginning to soften the angles of his
eyes, the idea suddenly had appeal. Why, since he was going to do a bit of drinking anyway, not take advantage of
whisky that would not only be better than he would buy,
but free.

This was what he asked himself, and when he had the
answer he said: "Sure. I'd like to."

He replaced the telephone gently, distance in his gaze as
his brain assimilated the things she had said. For it came
to him now that she was not the only one who needed help.
In his present mood he could use some himself. If they
could help each other for a little while, so much the better.

A NOTE ON THE TYPE

The text of this book is set in Caledonia, a Linotype face designed by W. A. Dwiggins, the man responsible for so much that is good in contemporary book design and typography. Caledonia belongs to the family of printing types called "modern face" by printers—a term used to mark the change in style of type-letters that occurred about 1800. It has all the hard-working feet-on-the-ground qualities of the Scotch Modern face plus the liveliness and grace that is integral in every Dwiggins "product" whether it be a simple catalogue cover or an almost human puppet.

4-2-58- 636

P. 25-35-50-59- 60 - 67-68 - 69 - 70
71 -73 - 74 - 76 - 90-91 -192 ☺ = 94 -
117 - 133 - 142 - 146 - 151 - 154 - 155 .

with commendable logic -